Joseph Sykes

Later Poems

Joseph Sykes

Later Poems

ISBN/EAN: 9783337241865

Printed in Europe, USA, Canada, Australia, Japan

Cover: Foto ©Andreas Hilbeck / pixelio.de

More available books at **www.hansebooks.com**

LATER POEMS:

BY

JULIO.

LONDON:
WHITTAKER AND CO., AVE MARIA LANE.

BRIGHTON:
THOS. PAGE, 173, NORTH STREET.
— — —
MDCCCLXXI.

PREFACE.

In a former Series of Poems the Author sought to portray the rehabilitation of fallen natures. Treated alike in the literal ("Never More") or symbolic method ("Fountain of Truth"), his ideal was found in the perfect equilibrium of physical and moral energy ("Philosophic Merchant").

In the concluding Series, although the volume is smaller, the range of thought will be found wider.

The "Scenes from Plutarch" may recall to the Reader some of those stories which made the heart beat faster in youthful days.

In the Didactic Poems, fragmentary as some are, the great problem of Death, as influencing different classes of minds, is dwelt upon at some length, yet more in a suggestive than descriptive way.

The Apothegms, as condensed thoughts in elegiac metre, may recall a great German model, which they cannot hope to rival (*Xenien*).

The Rhymed Compositions are extremely varied in character; but in all, even the two that at first sight seem entirely sensuous, the lesson is taught that a powerful nature will not be contented with the low range of merely sensual indulgences, but force itself upwards to purer regions of thought.

Brighton.
February, 1871.

CONTENTS.

CONTENTS.

PART I.

COMPOSITIONS IN CLASSIC METRES.

LATER POEMS.

PART I.

COMPOSITIONS IN CLASSIC METRES.

INTRODUCTORY TO SCENES
FROM PLUTARCH.

ILLUSTRIOUS guide to where the limits reach
    Of ancient story in the fields of fame;
We walk, with thee, beside Time's wreck-strewn
      beach—
    We weigh each action, and we spell each name.

Yet more we love thee, when the inner life
    Of those old days thy magic lines disclose:
We see the victor, when the battle's strife
    Has ceased, and weary Nature claims repose.

Those grand old times, girt by the glowing light
    Which fancy lends to the far distant view,

Are here revealed entire to mortal sight,
  And the romantic blends into the true.

Of Greece and Rome we see each magic form :
  The temple glowing with artistic fire ;
Of passion's conflict the far-sounding storm ;
  And hear the poet chant to golden lyre.

Ennobling fact for letters—he, who wrote,
  Scarce less illustrious on the world's wide page
Than those whose portraits we attentive note,
  Stands forth, historian of a mighty age.

To live for greatness is a noble task :
  To write of exploits till the reader's mind
Shall with great recital blend, and ask
  If Fate may not a like occasion find ;

This was old Plutarch's mission, and his book
  Has charmed the leisure of adventurous souls,
Whose spirits from the Past their impulse took,
  While victory's hymn from thousand voices rolls.

SCENES FROM PLUTARCH.

I.

ISADAS.

IN the war between Sparta and Thebes, as Plutarch
tells us, this youthful hero rushed from the bath
into the fight, without donning his defensive
panoply, and imposed such terror on the enemy,
that, deeming him a God, they gave way, and left
the Spartans masters of the field.* The late Sir
C. Eastlake illustrated this action by one of his
finest works, entitled "The Young Spartan."

Wild war rolls onward to the city walls ;
Hard pressed, the Spartans yield to hostile ranks ;
A weary fight seems near disastrous end.
But who comes rushing on, with spear in hand,
Devoid of vestment or defensive arms,

---

* *Vide* "Plutarch's "Agesilaus."

Fresh from the bath, in youth's rare beauty clothed—
Perfect in form, with fleetest turn of limb?
An aureole of light beams round his head—
His hair streams like trail of fire behind;
Fearless his mien, nor e'en the God of Fight
Looked more determined victory to win—
Yet, mixed with resolution's dauntless mien,
Bloomed in its spring-tide force the grace of youth.
" It is a God," spreads *now* from rank to rank :
" Th' Immortal comes from the Olympian hills,
" Jove sends him here to succour Sparta's sons."—
The foe gives way, and soon a panic spreads.
Again they shout, " A God has come to sight ;"
" Mars or Apollo combats on our side."
Godlike, in truth, —so rare it is to find
A noble soul with noble form allied,—
Too often doomed the opposite to see :
Fair face and figure joined to Devil's spite,
Or warlike head that masks a coward's heart.
But here was joined the bloom of beauty's flower
With fruit of earnest resolution's will !
Resolved in country's cause to win or die.

And so it issued; for where'er the youth
Pressed onward, all drew back, with fear possessed,
As though against immortal force they strove.
And so it was in truth, for strength divine
Lives in the firm determined will, that casts,
Not merely fear aside, but ev'ry thrall
Of selfish feelings bound to pleasure's chain;
Or that cold, creeping indolence that blights
Each gen'rous impulse ere it fruit can bear.
Not so Isadas: graced with faultless form,
Meet to win maiden's love, or be adored
With passion's flame in stolen rendezvous,
He risked his limbs, his mantling youthful blood,
To combat with his country's foes and fall,
A mangled corpse, on hard-contested field.

He was not destined so to end. The fight
Is o'er, and joyful sound of victory
Peals from the Spartan ranks; the city-gates
Fly wide; the sacrificial altar smokes;
With solemn joy the patriot youth is crowned,
And glad Laconia holds high festival.

So, to the end of time, historic page
Emblazons with bright hues the noble deed,—
By prompt, heroic action, vict'ry won !
Thrice-happy youth, who quick the moment seized,
When fortune grants a starting point for fame,
Prepared and ready,—for a brief delay,
And the occasion were for ever lost !
Thus promptitude to snatch the fated hour
Is half-way station to bright victory,
And makes the weakest mightier than their foes.
Example radiant as a lamp, to all
Who study the dead leaves of history—
Not as an irksome task, but there to find
The living records of man's restless force,
And blooming flower of high heroic deeds !

II.

CIMON'S DEATH.

THIS great Athenian, who with mighty deeds
    Had swayed the Council and great armies led
To victory o'er Barbarian and Greek,
For action and for eloquence renowned,
Dreamed, ere he started for his post once more,
A dog had bayed at him with human voice,
" I and my whelps will gladly see thee here ; "
And, at the solemn sacrifice, he saw
A swarm of ants cling to his foot and smear
His skin with blood,—a portent strange to all.
Yet shrunk not Cimon from wide-reaching plans,
Greece to avenge on the Barbarian hordes.
His fleet he led to Cyprus, and despatched
Some trusty messengers to Ammon's shrine,
Counsel to ask for furtherance of plans.
The God replied, " Go back ; he is with me ! "
Quick they returned, and, when they reached the camp,

They found their leader dead, and were apprized
It was the hour in which the Oracle
Declared, " He is with me ": marking the truth
That men, who with high gen'rous souls are blessed,
Are God-like in their essence and their frame,
And that an aureole of the Divine
Doth light the patriot to his glorious end.
For no less kind than great was Cimon's soul ;
He willing shared his table and his purse
With citizens whom fortune favour'd less.
Oft had his nature felt the glow of wine,
With genial impulse lighting up the heart ;
And beauty, too, had plunged his leisure hours
In passion's ebb and flow,—yet, above all,
His life was chained to duty, and he felt
His country's glory as his single aim.

—

III.

MARIUS'S REIGN OF TERROR.

IT was when carnage through the streets of Rome
   Revelled in slaughter of the citizens,
And unsubdued, capricious, worked its end :
The hoary Consul urging on his bands
Of slaves, who, armed, wrought out the instincts which
A life of servitude too often brings—
Oppressors and oppressed—the wheel that turns
In its gyrations round the circle brings
Of wrong and bloodshed, violence and crime—
A man there was who, in those troubled days
(Proscription flaunting in its blood-stained robe),
Had won applause and fame for gifts of speech,
Moulding the hearers to the speaker's will.
Antonius,* for bright eloquence renowned,
Too often 'gainst the tyrant now in power

---

* Grandfather of the Triumvir, Marc Antony.

Had fiercest accents hurled, pardon to win.
He refuge sought under a humble roof,
Where welcome hailed the richly-gifted guest.
Basely betrayed by one who sold him wine,
A troop was soon despatched to bring his head—
Mother of sarcasm and indignant speech.
The soldiers mounted to the victim's room ;
Their chief, one Annius, remained below.
A man unarmed is easy to despatch.
Yet none could do it : such the moving power
That Nature gave to eloquence and truth.
No history tells us how the Orator
Pleaded for life ; yet may we well suppose
Truth gave him accents in this latest hour
Fitted the rudest natures to subdue.
Perchance he told them of their native home
And tender magic of the household gods,
And of bright scenes of youth, when life appears
Like gushing fountain glitt'ring in the sun.
Ere slavery had brought its blight and curse.
Perchance he touched some chord that vibrates when
Man stands beside his fellow-mortal's form,

And rank shrinks back to shadow-line of death.

That was his triumph, mightier now than when

The Forum listened to impassioned speech.

For *now* his cause seemed won ; arms fell from
      hands,

Tears flowed from eyes, and faltering looks proclaimed

. Great Nature's protest 'gainst the lust of blood.

Thus found his followers their absent chief ;

But he, more cruel, did the deed himself,

And brought Antonius' head to Marius,

Who soon thereafter met a wretched doom.

IV.

INTERVIEW BETWEEN ALEXANDER THE GREAT AND THE BRACHMANS.

ON Alexander's return from his Indian expedition, he sent for ten of the Gymnosophists, or Brachmans, and propounded many interesting questions. He dismissed these learned men with magnificent presents.

Victorious chiefs pluck choicest fruits of life.
At their approach the captive Princess smiles,
And beauty follows on their army's march :
Nor less see they the notablest of men
In every country where their eagles fly.
Thus Alexander, after varied march
Through conquered Persia to the Indian shores,
Where never ship had sailed nor army trod,
Desired to converse hold with learned men,
In Brachman legend versed and Eastern lore.

The pupil of a Master great in fame,
Whose name and works have traversed ages down
To modern times—the mighty Stagyrite—
He, the great Captain, well might wish to know
What line of study Eastern thought pursued.
Perchance he deemed that something he might learn
Of Fate's decrees relating to himself!
The Sages came, and questions were discussed
With much of brevity, nor wanting wit :
The Earth's creation and Man's destiny—
What raises mortals o'er their fellows' heads,
And what may happen when death's summons calls.
An interview well worthy of our note ;
A peaceful episode mid scenes of war ;
An hour's brief converse ere the army marched !
Each went his way : the Conqueror to his task
Of marching o'er the prostrate necks of men,
Till he arrived on fair Chaldea's plain,
The allotted bound'ry of his meteor-course :
Destined no more the phalanx *thence* to lead,
Or to his native land triumphant come
With aureole of glory such as none

Had won since the first dawn of history.
The band of sages home returned, to teach
And guard the mystic emblems of a faith
Destined to rule o'er many an Eastern mind.
And, in his meditations on the world,
On busy life, and the decrees of Fate,
The Brachman, hearing of the Monarch's end,
Cut off in all the ardour of his youth,
Far from his native land, plans unachieved,
And no successor for his Empire's fame,
O'er frugal meal, in some sequestered spot,
Might deem himself more happy than the man
Whose panoramic march had awed the world.

This interview of warrior and sage,
Held on the confines of those famous lands,
Weighs more upon the springs of modern thought
Than all the victories by armies gained.
One gives the triumph of material force,
And skilful leadership directing all ;
The other brings us to the sphere of mind,
Exerting influence on the human race,

And bending nations to a certain creed.

The ancient Brachman faith preserved its sway

Erect amidst the universal crash

Of thrones and dynasties throughout the world !

The Macedonian conqueror lay dead :

His empire crumbled into fragments—broke.

That Eastern faith struck deep its roots, and lives

E'en to our day, in its symbolic rites,—

A lasting conquest o'er the mind of man.

v.

ARCHIMEDES AT SYRACUSE.

PHILOSOPHERS, 'tis said, oft dwell apart,
    Nor mingle in the crowded marts of life,
Retiring from their kind in solitude,
Encompassed by the forms of abstract thought—
Yet some have made the highest science stoop
To daily wants of men, constructing bridge
That spans the torrent, and from height to height
Conducts the child or timid invalid,
With other marvels of the engineer.
And thus, in olden times, when Nature's laws
Were by man's intellect but half-explained,
A great philosopher, whose name has come
On roseate cloud of fame down to our day,
Defended Syracuse against a host,
Not of barbarian tribes, or Asia's slaves,
But Roman legions, led by one whom all
Proclaimed the greatest Captain of his day—

Marcellus, sword of Rome and Carthage's dread.
O mighty power of genius!   Vainly strove
The legions to approach that city's walls,
Or with the galleys landing to effect.
Launched in mid air, rock-showers their circles traced,
Then thund'ring crushed the assailants' serried ranks,
And swamped the vessels ere they touched the shore,
Or bore them quivering high above the host.

The Roman leader, vexed, yet not dismayed,
Came nearer, hoping to avoid the stroke
Of such projectiles by a bending course.
But vain his care ; for Archimedes now
Brought other engines to the city's walls,
And, near, as far, rained death among the host.

Oft have men said, that one great leader's mind
Is worth ten thousand men in battle strife,
When hosts contend for palm of victory.
But here, for once in the world's history,
A single brain outweighed collected force,
Led by the greatest warrior of his age.

Sum up these figures, and discern how great
The glory was of Syracuse's defence.
And yet 'tis said this man of abstract thought
Deemed all the glory of accomplished facts
But trifling, when compared with problems' truth,
By delicate deductions clearly proved,
And stored in science' treasure-house for aye.
Thought is a monarch, mightier in its force
Than all the potentates that men adore,—
Immeasurable in its greatness, vast,
Nor deigning always visibly to work.
Yet here it served the patriot's purpose well,
And gave immortal glory to the man,
Who perfected this scheme of bold defence !
He died, 'tis said, whilst bending o'er his task,
Marshalling quantities in order close,
By geometric lines a world enclosed.
A Roman soldier, with his brutal sword,
Cut short the thread of those far-reaching thoughts.

Not so Marcellus wished; his gen'rous soul
Had longed with Archimedes to converse

And honour pay to Science' greatest son.
His end all men might envy, for it came
With sudden severance of mind from clay :
The lifeless trunk lay mid the scholar's work,
Where geometric lines in sand were traced ;
His soul's ethereal essence mounted high
To spheres of thought all boundless and sublime.

*   *   *   *

Engraved with forms of cylinder and sphere,
His tomb proclaimed the great geometer.
A century had passed ; the savant's grave
'Mid newer interests neglected lay.
When a great Roman to Sicilia came :
The orator whose glowing page remains,
Instinct with life, the scholar's heritage ;
The Quæstor * found at length the pillar where,

---

* Cicero's Quæstorship. The young Orator sought for and
restored the neglected tomb.

With weeds o'er grown, inscription half effaced,
Yet still with sphere and cylinder intact,
The great philosopher's remains were laid.
Doubtless he gazed with reverence on the spot,
For genius holds a chain of finest links,
Binding in unison illustrious souls,
In spite of ages' wreck and spoils of time.
Two thousand years have passed; the names of both
Live in the memory of a grateful world—
Undying heritage for latest times.

*   *   *   *

VI.

TIMOLEON.

TIMOLEON of Corinth had an elder brother, whose life he had saved. Timophanes was turbulent and ambitious. Entrusted with military command, he abused his trust, and sought to enslave his native city. After every persuasion had been tried in vain, Timoleon allowed two of his friends to slay his brother, for which he was cursed and shunned by his mother. Timoleon remained many years without taking any part in public affairs; at last he consented to lead an expedition for the freedom of Sicily, which he happily accomplished.

Great citizen of Corinth, on thy brow
A patriot's glory rests, e'en in that hour
When guilty brother's life was sacrificed,
Rather than thy free city be enslaved.
Act of dread import! None should lightly judge

Of such a struggle in a noble mind :
The ties of blood by higher claims subdued,
And citizenship before kindred placed.
'Twas not for selfish ends that deed was done.
Efforts were made to bring him back to right;
To Corinth's liberties his life was due.
Yet none can thus o'erstep great Nature's laws
Nor suffering escape. A mother's curse
Rung in Timoleon's ears for many a year
And doomed him to inaction, whose large mind
And steadfast will for leadership had marked.
Saw he a spectre in his hours of rest,
That o'er his shoulder looked with steadfast eyes ?
Or was it self-inflicted punishment
For having served his country but too well ?
Sufficient 'tis that twenty years flew by
Whilst Corinth's greatest son inactive stood,
Nor mingled in the press of citizens.
How passed those years we know not; from his life
Bright manhood's days were taken, and he stood,
Like mighty pillar, silent but erect.
His life might thus have ended, and his name,

Never engraved on history's sculptured stone,
Attesting greatness for a future age,
Have fallen, like quenched torch, in sea of time.
But not so willed the Fates.   His hour arrived:
Public necessity proclaimed the man
To lead an army where Sicilia groaned
Beneath oppression's foul and galling yoke.
And now came triumph,—not the victory
In tyrant's cause against a rival host;
But for a nation's life, by foes oppressed—
Traitors within and enemies without.
Timoleon vanquished both.   The citizens,
The struggle ended, hailed him as their chief:
No vulgar chief, astride o'er prostrate men,
But ruling by his virtues' influence.

The greatest man on fair Sicilia's shore,
He found a country, friends, a second home.
Here rolled in golden waves the years that fate
Allotted to the patriot-citizen.
His noble form above his fellows tow'red:
For virtue eminent—not for the arts

That win obedience, or make fast a throne.
With glowing characters his name was writ,
In fairest outline, on the scroll of Time.
And did the parent who had cursed him once,
And blighted for long years ambition's flower—
Did she, a ghost on dreary Pluto's shore,
Catch but an echo from the world of life,
And feel the greatness of her glorious son ?

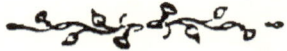

FRAGMENTS OF A DRAMATIC POEM.

"BOUND BY AN OATH."

Scene I.—THE PRINCE FABRIZIO, in his Cabinet.

A M I as once I was ?   If not, what change
    Resides in words, whose echoes now are gone,
Girt by some forms of speech ?   Can such control
A man's career, through all his future life
Shaping his will, as with an iron grasp ?
Whence come these scruples ?   Did I feel them when
Obstacles crossed ambition or caprice—
Solid advancement or bright pleasure's dream ?
No ; to such yieldings I have been as bronze.
But *now*, when gazing from the topmost tower
Of life's fair edifice, compacted strong—
Lustrous without, and well-contrived within—
I pause and quake, and bow myself before

The phantom of my spoken words.   'Tis so.
Somewhat within me urges to obey :
It *was* an oath—my kinsman's parting glance,
Soothed by my promise, seemed all bathed in light.
Shall I, then, bring it back, with vengeance filled,
To haunt my dreams and dog my daily steps ?
Unto this potent voice I needs must yield,
E'en at the sacrifice of cherished plans.

＊　　　　＊　　　　＊　　　　＊

Yet to have wrought for others—to remove
Each obstacle that ministers to their success—
To make their victory easy, and myself
Shrink into littleness !   'Tis somewhat strange.
Yes, I remember well the fatal day
When Luigi, near his end, bid me come close,
And thus addressed me with his failing breath :—
" You will succeed, my cousin, to a State
Not large in territory, but which holds
A certain balance 'midst the neighbouring Powers.
Compact it should be, and devoid of strife.

One haughty noble has defied my will,

And plotted ceaselessly against my throne.

I could have crushed him, but have still refrained

Because his father saved my life when young.

You know him well, and when your reign begins,

Doubtless you'd strike him down,—yet you must spare

And leave his guilt unpunished.   If my soul

May rest at peace, its latest wish fulfilled,

Swear you will do it, and I'll bless you when

All earthly objects from my view recede."

I took the oath : my kinsman died in peace.

(Five years later.)

Scene II.—Room in a Castle.   FABRIZIO on a Couch.

I may live longer ; but I scarcely think

Life's treasure-chest holds much I care to see ;

'Tis worn-out lumber—cumbrous yet not strong.

One wish, so often thwarted, still survives.

Impulse may reach a certain height, but then
The drooping energies no more sustain
Our flickering purpose to its destined end.
Yes; good and evil fortune have been mine,
Like rays of light that from stained windows fall,
With varied colours, on Time's dusty floor.
At Fortune's deeds I have no cause to rail ;
But at my faltering purpose when the flood
Bore high my bark above the swelling waves ;
For, crippled by an oath too rashly sworn,
I let another win the glitt'ring prize,
Whilst my own hands shaped out his victory—
Like some old libertine, who leads a girl
To fair fruition's brink and leaves her there,
Throbbing with new unsatisfied desires,
To fall before some vigorous lover's will.

(*He goes to the window*).

   •   •   •   ✳

Aye, let me see once more my banner float,
Heraldic glories glittering in the sun,

And shadow cast from massive castle walls.
The insects' hum the only sound that breaks
The stillness of this lovely summer's day.
That will decline at eve, when sunlight fades.
And so declines my life; but worse than this
Most natural decay of worn-out frame,
Is to relinquish my long-nurtured plan,
To vindicate my name, so long obscured,—
Suspected of a double crime, yet pure.
But one year more, and all might have been well:
Proofs clear as light delivered to my friends,
And foes confounded by their evidence.
But *now*, a year is long for one so weak;
Soon will the glory of September fade,
And Autumn's mellow days be quenched in mist,
With chilly damps that drown the flame of life.
No; I shall never see the coming year;
Nor will my fame, like yonder climbing sun,
Surmount the clouds that veiled its early beams.
'Tis easy to depart with wish fulfilled,
Plans that have won success's radiant crown,
Success that tinges all the clouds of life

With its own vivid lustre ; but to die
With dislocated projects, hopes o'erthrown,—
So near the bourne of victory to have
My fancies scattered and my fame obscured.
Oh ! this is bitter, and I curse the oath,
Made by my kinsman's bed, to spare that man.
He never felt the tie of gratitude,
But, with the cringing meanness of a cur,
Plotted yet more against the man by whom
His life was spared, and traversed all my plans,
And soon will triumph at my speedy end.
One chance remains ! *(To a servant.)* " Send for
     Antonio,"
Who executes my will like Nubian slave,
Mute, quick, yet cautious, with untiring zeal,—
He shall this message to the city bear,
Which may forestall the triumph of my foes,—
Slave to my oath, the victim of my word,
Fate owes my truth this final recompense.

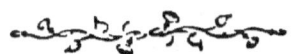

DIDACTIC SERIES.

I.

SOME who have talents, fortune, leisure-time—
 Those puissant levers social mass to raise—
Leave, at the close of life, no deeper trace
Than ripples by a stone in waters cast !
Down life's swift stream they drift, with careless mien,
Nor cross its current to the safer shore,
Nor force the obstacle of floating weeds.
Their strivings, intermittent, let the stream
Bear them away : and they at length exclaim—
" Struggles are useless—Fate has so decreed ;"—
For this sad doctrine of fatality
A most convenient mantle throws o'er sloth.
Youth, act not so ; but, as the Poet taught—
That fine old Roman—in his vigorous verse* :—
Aim thou at somewhat : let thy arrow strike
Some mark defined, high o'er the head of crowds.

---

* Persius, *Sat.* 3, *v.* 60.

D

II.

VIRTUS VIRILIS.

IS courage virtue? Yes, the Romans said,—
    For the same words in the old Latin tongue
Express both meanings,—and we often find,
That want of courage leads to error's blight.
'Tis this which makes the faltering child deceive;
In after-years it frames the school-boy's lie;
And the Collegian, when his bills fall due,
Lets slip the moment to avow his fault,
And drags through weary years the chain of debt.
Are you courageous? "What!" some fiery blade
Exclaims; "am I not prompt to brawl or fight?"
And, with a graver mien, another asks,
"Will I not name and honour vindicate
From all reproach 'gainst those who would assail?"
Softly, my friend; courage is oftest shown
In moral struggles with perplexing facts.
To tell a woman we no longer love

Is one óf these most difficult to meet;

For then she weeps, and with her tears there comes

Some long-forgotten charm, that casts its spell,

And half brings back the love of other days,

With torture of irresolution's whirl.

Or she bursts forth in rage, and in the gleam

That flashes sudden from her lustrous eyes,

We feel the tide of passion rolling back,

Just when a yawning gulph betwixt us lies.

Or, when a friend, with wealth and talents, yields

To the insidious flatterer's evil voice,

And with good-natured impulse ruin seeks—

To try to bring him back, offending one,

Who often has advantaged our career,

Here is the courage of a noble mind,

Braving all dangers for a worthy end.

Again, impulsive natures often say,

When borne upon excitement's rolling tide,

(Or unstrung nerves, after a sleepless night,

Reverse the true perspective of our lives,)

Words, they would give a treasure to annul—

But pride forbids their footsteps to retrace.

True courage then steps forward, and at once,
(A nobler sacrifice than life or wealth)
Confesses all its errors, and declares
That transient mists have veiled the sun of truth,
And, humbled before error's heritage,
Pardon and counsel for the future seeks.
And so we find the ancient Romans right;
Another debt we owe to classic lore.

III.

"MORS JANUA VITÆ."

IT may be well to die, to quit at once
    This sea of trouble with its bitter waves,
And be emancipated from the thrall
That course of added years so surely brings.
But to lie languishing for many a day—
Supine on couch, so active once of limb,
To watch the ebb on life's storm-beaten shore,—
And bit by bit to sink into the tomb,
Far from the scenic pageantry of life,
And equilibrium of digestion's power,
Diffusing vigour through each well-knit limb,—
Oh ! *this is sad*, whilst phantom forms intrude—
Some girt with mem'ries of the joyous lights
That o'er the path of life serenely shone ;
But others fraught with recollections sad,
Of shattered hopes and happiness destroyed—
Of pleasure madly won at cost of calm ;

For oft the tree of knowledge bears a fruit
So bitter to the taste, that we would give
All we possess not to have plucked the branch
That hung so tempting by the wand'rer's path.
All this, repeated hourly by our couch,
Like tick of clock that jars upon the ear,
Is still accompanied by wearing pain,
That mocks all efforts to avert its sting.
Friends come and go, perchance with anxious mien,
And bland hypocrisy of " better hopes,"—
Knowing full well that soon the end will come.
The table's strewed with phials, on the chance
Of some hours' respite from unceasing pain.
Through window's pane no cheerful light appears,
But fog and grime in equal portions rise ;
Whilst priest and doctor in succession try,
With creed or medicine, to allay unrest.
O, let me die beneath the vault of heaven !
Kissed by the winds—soothed by perfume of flowers—
With parting glance bent on the massive forms
Of forest, gilded by the western ray :
Not far, perchance, from the ancestral halls—

The fields and grove that saw our boyhood's sports,
So, when the circle of our destiny
Is filled, we may on earth's fair bosom rest,
Returning back to Nature's ample fold.

*   *   *   *

How fares it with the thought of death 'mid scenes
Of busy life's excitement, and the roll
Of stormy passions beating on Time's shore ?
Some seek to mask such thoughts with wine and
    flowers.
Unwelcome vision 'tis to minds of most;
Yet, when digestion's power is low, 'twill come
After excess, fatigue, or the collapse
Of cherished schemes, which bring amid their fall
A certain sense of instability.
Yet others cherish the remembrance, like
A cloud that breaks monotony of blue :
A certain luxury they find in thoughts
Of that mysterious power, the Leveller
Of great and mighty, beautiful and brave.

Some seek all contrasts with an artist's zest :
From splendid feasts in lamp-lit halls, where mirth
Entwines its wreath round beauty's radiant brow,
They love to pass to lonely churchyard's graves,
Caressing oft the vision of repose,
Whose monumental stone is girt by flowers.

＊   ＊   ＊   ＊

Yet, shunned or welcome, still the vision lies
Around us and above us and beneath.
All Nature speaks of life's embrace with death,
And fresh existence springing from the tomb.
All Nature tells us we must one day die,
And life's uncertainty bears in its womb
An element of grandeur for us all.
To-day, to-morrow, in a score of years,
The scene will change, but none can tell how soon
The great perspective of a wider world
Shall dawn conclusive on our sharpened sense.

IV.

WHAT are the goods of life? a question oft
    Demanded, rarely answered as we wish.
Friendship? Yes, that may give us moments when
We feel a glow that brightens all around,
And glory in negation of ourselves.
Pursuit of knowledge? Aye, a lofty gate,
That opens wider as the advancing mind
Is braced for stronger efforts, and resolves
The Halls to enter, where concentred thought
And ripe experience of past ages dwell!
Health, too, is good; untiring energy,
By equilibrium of nature poised,
That seems from toil fresh nourishment to draw.
A fair external presence, when the mind
Shines through transparent shell of beauty's form.
A voice to pierce the crowd and charm its ear.
'Tis good to own a mind that soars above
The world of slander, so that not a drop
Of its foul venom e'er can stain your robe.

Good to have faith in higher lives of men,
Who tread self-interest down beneath their feet;
Good to be freed from superstition's chain,
Which founds its creed on coward fears of men;
Good to believe that others *may* be right,
When most they differ from our cherished views;
'Tis good to battle for a noble cause,
Though certain to be vanquished, and have faith
In Time's redressing power for future days;
Good to rise active with the early morn,
Nor tire till sombre eve her twilight sends,
With steady energy, progressing still
Through occupation's ever-changing scene.
Is love a good? a question difficult
To solve or answer, since so many thoughts
Are bound up in that word, like separate flowers,
Forming a nosegay, thickly set with thorns.
Yet, we may say at once, that few desire
Through life to walk without affection's light.
To many a youth the passions in their train
Bring all the evils that can life afflict—
Rage, envy, jealousy, remorse, despair,

Annihilation of the tranquil mind,
Unfitness for pursuits of active life,
Insensibility to smaller joys.
Sleep flies their couch ; the healthy appetite
Is gone ; they crave for ceaseless stimulants,
Whilst reeling from intoxication worse
Than wine or spirits e'er produced in man.
Passion leads on to crime.   Some deed is done,
In moments when the mind control has lost,
Which dooms us to the cypress avenue,
Where man walks sadly to remorseful end,
And ever-following sees a spectre form.
Or, if our reason keeps us back from blood,
Or scruples of a timid nature's fears,
We thoughtless enter on the flowery slope
That downward leads, as *credit* opens wide
The fatal door, where, through enchanted halls,
Deluded victims to their doom descend,
And syren's smile by load of debt is bought.

*   *   *   *

All fall not so.   On some affection beams,

Girt with the purest light of tenderness
And noble thoughts, incentive to great deeds.
To such, love proves a blessing and a boon.
But these are few ; whilst victims of deceit,
Unruly passion, furious jealousy,
Maimed, scorched, and helpless, throng around life's
    path.

v.

MISTAKES ! Aye, tell me who doth not, at times,
    Forsake the true, for error's glittering path ?
Yet Nature, by her kindly laws, provides
That error's self oft leads back to the true :
Bearing us scathed, but cautious, on the flood
Of self-denial's waves to safer port.
Then, to the pilgrim, will occur again
A turning point in life—whose crisis leads
Back to the mount of virtuous resolve.
But some mistakes are fatal, and their sway
Leads down a steep incline to certain doom :
No footstep mounts again, no thought can rise,
To clearer atmosphere of former years.
Gone are those visions of the pure and good—
That rainbow arch that links our earth to heaven—
That sentiment of virtue which, in minds
Where stricter principles no longer sway,
Dwells with its hallowing presence, and conceals
The naked selfishness of daily life—

Veiling, like clustering ivy's freshest green,
The spectral phantom of satiety.
Then, habit, winding yet another coil,
Crushes the victim in its Python folds.
The avaricious, cruel, lustful man,
With age's leprous crust on brighter thoughts,
Lives but for evil, till his doom be sealed.

      *   *   *   *

Others, less guilty, own scant wish for good.
What hopes that elder man from years to win?
Where reach his longings in their fullest scope?
Some joys of sense: digestion's pleasing task,
With cheery friends, o'er the grape's choicest juice;
The illusions of the stage—the dancer's pose;
A lovely woman near, with toilette that
Excites the envy of the crowd below;
The neatest equipage—the choicest hack—
In park or Champs Elysées to be seen:
All purchasable goods in life's vast mart.

Some riches added to a gathered heap ;
A family connection, sweet to pride ;
Success o'er rivals on the crowded stage,
Where politics are made life's comedy,
And party's fragments hail him as their chief.

   *   *   *   *

All this he hopes for ; but to work for good—
Extinguish some foul influences that veil,
Like smoke, the sunny aspects of our world—
For this, how few will labour, or desire
To see corruption flying from the light !

VI.

HOW often exercise and study yield
     But scanty fruit, if heedlessly pursued.
The one fatigues, the other crams the mind
With crude and undigested facts, that leave
No stores of wisdom for our onward path.
Aimless we live, by passion's chain enthralled,
By fitful study's claim at times subdued.
Thus, when the year its sweeping course has closed,
Time's round by mere futilities is marked:
Our dial-plate has but one shadow's line.
None of those questions, whose gigantic form
Moves solemnly across Time's level floor:
Collapse of war; repeal of penal laws,
Which take from man the life which Heaven bestowed;
Extinction of the hopeless pauper's class:
That later creed embracing all the rays
From lights held o'er the march of progress swift;
Love pointing to fraternity of man,

And great hereafter framed by higher powers,—
None of these questions, of horizon large,
Can dwell in minds whose circling course is filled
By petty cares and pleasures of to-day,
And selfishness, that ever grooves its path
With deeper indent on the plane of life.

E

VII.

THE thought of Death, how acts it on the mind?
　　Did the old Roman realise its force,
Whom constant precepts. like a spur in flank
Of sluggish horse, exhorted to be brave?
In truth, men fear not death in common life,
Because they think not of it: appetite,
And vigorous digestion's healing power,
Sending fresh blood through ev'ry quickened pulse,
With other appetites that wait on health—
Ambition's restless schemes and pleasure's whirl—
Keep at a distance that grim phantom-shape.
With others, too, the struggle how to live
From day to day excludes all future thought.
But modern thought delights to analyze
What superstition's chains so long enthralled—
Linked to some dread futurity of pain.
"Be orthodox or damned:" such was the cry
Each Church sent forth through ages' gloomy space.
So came upon the mind a numbing fear,

Not of extinction, but of endless woe,

Darkening with gloom the classic formula.

But freer thought has chased away these forms,

Placing instead the consciousness of Love—

Diviner essence—governing the world,

And voice of pardon sounding through all space.

Yet truly said Rousseau,* that wicked men,

Such as, without one grain of moral sense,

Outrage the laws of Nature and of God,

Are most embarrassing to finer thoughts—

In this and future life most hard to fit.

Some punishment would needful seem for such,

To supplement defects in human laws,

Which strike not always the most guilty head.

Yet not for ever : for eternal pain

Destroys the highest image we can form

Of all-embracing goodness in a God.

*   *   *   *

Spite of philosophy, Death's shadow will

---

* " Les méchans sont bien embarassans, et dans ce monde et dans l'autre."—*Confessions.*

Extend its outline on the plain of life,
And cast a chill at times o'er vigorous man,
When thought conducts him to that bound'ry line.
And few of older years, though life would seem
But colourless and tame, wish to depart
On that great journey through vast halls of space.

———

VIII.

OLD Age and Death, two lofty pillars, stand
     On life's vast plain, strewed with the wrecks of Time,
Far where the dim horizon slopes away,
And misty vapours veil the orange sky ;
Grey is one pillar, and the other black,—
Black with an underlying layer of light,
That trembles 'neath the polished marble's grain.
As maimed and feeble mortals pass the *first*
Of these two columns, some grow faint and halt,
Viewing the faces of companions dear
All changing into that grey, ashy hue,
And lamentation's wail from some is heard !
But, when the *second* pillar comes to view,
The crowd is silent, as though some deep thought
Concealed the words ere they could pass the lips ;
For through the folds of darkness lurid beams
Necessity, and all must bow before
That revelation of man's destiny.
Age may be wept ; to Death we must incline,
As to the ultimate and final goal,

Whither flow on the varied streams of life—
The waving banners, and the pageantry
Of long procession marching to its doom.
Some narrow creeds may teach, when life expires,
The gate swings wide to everlasting pain ;
But higher view of true divinity,—
Inductions from a mighty group of facts,
And, more than these, the instinct of our hearts,
Pointing to goodness as the golden chain
That binds the All in its harmonious course,—
Assuages fears like these, and bids us hope
For exercise of higher faculties,
And happiness from well-accomplished work,
On slope of future worlds that glow with light,
'Mid music which no jarring note disturbs,
As now, where crime and misery prevail,
And blur our dismal light with shadows foul.
Our later years in contemplation rich,
The fiery passions crouching in repose,
May well prepare us for the final scene,
And be accepted with deep gratitude,
As balm and solace for a restless mind.

IX.

WAS his career a failure ?   He had won
    Some popular applause—some woman's love,
Aided the struggling, succoured the distressed,—
Yet all was done in fitful, careless guise,
Nor plan defined to which man's strivings reach.
And so he failed, when fifty years were past,
To leave his mark upon the scroll of time.
And then, on failure followed discontent,—
A morbid craving for the exceptional,
For elevation without ladder-steps,
Success without the labour it exacts.
Too active, he, to trifle hours away
With cards, or drive the polished balls along.
Too true by Nature not to feel contempt
For fashion's hard-earned service, and a life
That holds few moments man can call his own.
He relished, too, in all, the natural,—
The brightly-beaming sun, the hour of eve—
When western sky is dyed with gorgeous hues—

The breezy morn, when traveller awakes,
New portions of earth's surface to explore;
Or, when in library the fire is lit,
To read of travels till the story grows
A branch from stem of the own student's thought.
Ambition's disenchantments then forgot,
He scanned the panorama of the world—
Its diverse races, and their customs strange,
Teaching that none should abstract rules exact,
Or bind his fellows to one mode of thought;
Reflecting, too, that those who win success
Oft bear the scars that tell of painful strife,
And relish lose for Nature's simple fare,—
Or senses claim their debt, and man awakes
To find himself enslaved by some caprice,
Exacting tribute from the higher life.

x.

A PORTRAIT.

ACTIVE in intellect, not wholly strong,
  Soaring at times on Fancy's outstretched wing—
He was not of those firm-compacted men,
Moulded in bronze, who work with arm untired,
And e'en in pleasure show unfailing strength.
Oft times he could not sleep,—the slightest noise,
Some ripple of excitement in his mind
Condemned him to long vigils in his bed ;
At morn to rise, with haggard, weary face,
Each nerve on edge after a wakeful night.
And so, in higher things, his mind excursed
O'er widest range of Literature and Art ;
And now and then his hand a picture traced,
Charming the eye by graceful line and form,
Yet leaving no deep impress on the mind.
Pleasure he loved, draped in decorum's robe—
Not quite unmingled with the joys of sense,
Nor such resigned when age its mantle cast

On sloping shoulders and ungarnished head.
'Twas habit more than impulse that impelled;
But habit left him somewhat pleasure's slave.
Cheerless is life's decline, when ev'ry year
Consumes some portion of our cherished joys,
Leaving the mind more restless in its wants—
The frame more weighty and the step less free;
When no new interests compensate the loss,
The worshipped Goddess now retiring far,
Woo'd with constraint and hardly won at last:
An hour of joy followed by weary days,
With sinking spirits and oft-broken rest,
As reason finds the lamp of jealous thought
Pointing to wrinkled brow and cumbrous frame,
Eyes dimmed by age, and steps that falter *now*,
Nor mount again the courser loved of old
For chase, or promenade in field or park.
Yet still he loves to meet a woman's smile,
Especially when pearly teeth she shows,
Fair rounded arm, and hand that yields to touch,
White fingers, shapely, flexible yet strong,
On which contrasted gems their lustre show—

A diamond here, blended with sapphire's light,
Emerald and ruby in symmetric row,
With golden circle to complete the whole.
'Tis then he feels the rush of passion rise,—
Not, as of old, o'erflowing torrent's bed,
And bearing obstacles on foaming flood;
But gurgling feebly 'neath steep banks, where flowers
Bloom rarely on the arid, sun-cracked soil.

*   *   *   *

" O list to wisdom's voice," the Preacher cries,
" And wisely use the remnant of your days."
But other teachers whisper, " Life is short;
" Cull, then, the flowers that bloom Time's stream beside.
" But few remain—be happy whilst you can,
And once again with pleasure's wreath be crowned."

*   *   *   *

'Twixt counter promptings wavers many a mind,
Turning to one, and then to the other side :

A little pleasure,--then some serious thought,--
Till Time its knell with brazen clangour sounds,
That ends, by force, uncertainty and doubt,
And leaves the world with one poor trifler less.

Yet to our elder man not so it chanced :
Something yet stirred beneath the crust which years
Depose on the fast petrifying mind.
He scorned the cynic's disbelief in good,
Holding that millions of our toiling race
Were passing over stern endeavour's mount
To where the plain with widening view expands,
And brighter suns beam on the ripening grain :
Where glorious sheaves reward the reaper's toil,
And freshest pastures eager herds invite,
Whilst happy families are sheltered well,
And smiling faces peep from workman's door.
How sad such thoughts should ever be obscured
By fleeting pleasures of our lower sense,
Which down to muddy levels drag the mind—
To stagnant pools in place of mountain spring.
Yet it is often so : and habits formed

Groove their deep path for man's declining years.

*   *   *   *

Judge not our brother harshly : rather hope
That such soiled vestments have been thrown aside
Long ere the voice of death breathed in his ear.

XI.

THE BURLINGTON ARCADE.

WHERE Piccadilly's roar booms on the ear
    With endless stream of omnibus and cab,
And smarter vehicles that glance between
The pond'rous dray and slowly-moving cart,
A Gallery its shops attractive shows
In long perspective, with bright jets of gas.
On days of rain it welcome shelter gives
To tired pedestrian with mud-stained boots,
Or country swell, come to see *life in Town.*
Here is reflected much of what the time
To curious observer gives for thought;
Bright shops display their glitt'ring store of goods,
And flaunting women not too bashful walk,
Inviting gaze of idle passer-by.
As life abounds in contrasts ever new,
The farther end of this prolonged Arcade
Abuts on buildings of palatial mien,
Temples of high and philosophic thought

For future years in Britain's capital.

So, like a stream between two mighty seas,—

One ever agitated by the winds,

The other sleeping in unvaried calm,—

This Gallery conducts the wanderer

And charms his senses as he onward goes,

From pole to pole of varied London life.

A certain neatness reigns : men leave *without*

The soiled and hurried air of business-life.

Here we may meditate and leisure find

To glance by turns from present to the past ;

'Tis something, too, to leave the ceaseless grind—

That torture to the delicate in frame—

Which haunts our busy streets throughout the day.

To this bazaar of human interests

Come country swell and raw unpracticed youth,

To find temptation smiling at their side.

The elder man of pleasure from his Club,

Seeking an appetite for evening meal,

May find some reflex of his former joys

As Phryne and her sisters pass along.

But higher thoughts to other breasts will come,

Who dream of times when error's ways no more
Shall tempt, but *all* bask in the light of truth :
No courtezan then left—no skulking thief,
Seeking to filch his neighbour's goods or fame ;
No sleek projector with his bubble scheme,
Entrapping the unwary with the bait
Of cent. per cent. in coming dividend ;
No brutal drunkards serpentine the street,
Or cruel master makes his home a hell,
And grudges his dependents' hard-earned bread.

Such thoughts rose in my mind but yesterday.
I saw the glorious reign of good and truth,—
All virtuous and happy,—when a girl
Hailed me in passing with a wanton glance.
Alas ! the reign of good not yet is come.
I left the Gallery with saddened mind,
Nor gained good spirits till the dinner-hour
Made life once more appear in colours bright.

20th December, 1869.

XII.

UNCERTAIN—yes, his mind kept halting, where
    A breath may turn to one or other side—
Blows it from Self-denial's rugged mount,
    It swiftly wafts us into Virtue's port;
If from Sloth's perfumed bed of ease it comes,
    Down sinks the man into the deepworn rut,
Grooved by the wheels of habit or of vice.

    No more for him the bracing breeze of morn
With plan of action for the well-filled day;
    No ever-widening prospect as he goes,
    Brings him the joy of obstacles o'ercome;
But daily sinking deeper in the mire,
    No more he rises from the couch of sloth,
But creeps irresolute to evil end.

*   *   *   *

How many wail over unhappy fate,

As though their weakness did not forge the bolt.
But stronger natures mutely fall or rise,
   Their noiseless steps are ever pressing on ;
Nor secret thoughts to other breasts confide—
   But leave the world to give its verdict when
The end has come, and all their plans revealed.

ELEGIACS.

EPIGRAMS AND APOTHEGMS.

I.

WHERE is temptation, we ask? Say rather, where
  is *our weakness?*
Some are tempted by gold, others by beautiful eyes;
Some lose sight of the good for want of a single
  endeavour,
Others by doing too much, active for all but the true.

II.

Two stars shine on our birth; when one is extinguished,
  the other
Dimmer and dimmer will grow, till it is lost to our view.
When their lustre is gone, man sinks in the billows of
  ocean,—
Honour's the name of one; that of the other is *Truth.*

III.

Yes, we are orthodox quite; we've got at the truth,
    and we know it.
Is there but *one* star in Heaven? shines its sun only
    on thee?

IV.

Many can tolerant seem, and let men go on life's
    errand;
Only in this they compel: how to approach unto God.

V.

When the monarch demanded what gift he should offer
    the wise man,
" Only," the latter replied, " out of my sunshine to go."
True, and the chiefest boon the State can give to the
    worker,
Is to leave at his choice freedom to speak and to act.

VI.

Every poet will think his verses are better than others;
Where, then, oh critics! declare, where is there room
    for the bad?

Every critic believes that he alone has the mission

Crowns to distribute, and praise, properly mingled with
blame,—

But the public, in truth, has judged for itself in the
matter ;

Author and critic alike follow their master's behest.

VII.

Love in its dawning is sweet; both youth and maiden
are certain

Fortune smiles on their path; none can be happy as
they ;

But when years are elapsed, and naught remains but
to quarrel,

Husband and wife declare Cupid a trickster at best.

VIII.

Travel is pleasant, 'tis said; but look at the group who
are wrangling

Over their bill at the inn, vowing they'll never
return.

Weary at home, men find that weariness follows on
    travel.
Surely the reason is plain,—is it not part of them-
    selves?

IX.

Where is the mortal who deems his judgment never
    can falter ?
Is he not here at his Club, looking through window at
    life ?
Hollow and vain he declares are all the hopes that we
    cherish ;
'Tis so to him, for, in truth, hollow is all in his heart.

X.

Let us be quick to get rich, for life so rapidly passes ;
Buy up the Company's shares,—premiums sure to be
    ours ;
Company smashes, and then we think, when too late,
    of the fable,
Tortoise and hare who run, but 'tis the slowest that
    wins.

XI.

" Wicked and fallen you were," the Preacher said to
    his hearers,

" But, by the action of grace, *now* you are happy and
    good."

Just at that moment a lad extracting from a pocket a
    purse,

Sotto voce replies, " Yees ; I be 'appy to-night."

XII.

" Ah, my dear fellow, 'tis true the women are all at my
    bidding ;

Seldom passes a day but I have notes from the fair."

Surely our friend forgets how oft his notes he ex-
    changes ;

Only his banker knows how many cheques he has
    drawn.

XIII.

Would you an orator be and sway men's minds at your
    pleasure ?

Learn in speaking to feel all that to others you say.

Would you as poet excel and reach Art's loftiest
summit?

Study the boundary line 'twixt the ideal and fact.

Men would you lead?　First try to probe the feelings
of others,

Till at the last you can say, "All that is human I've felt."

XIV.

When man is young, he should know that age may
some day o'ertake him—

Deference show to the wise, and to the head that is
grey.

When he is old, he should think how the young may
best be made happy,

Plunging himself for a time into the fountain of youth.

XV.

Wisest is he who feels that wisdom oft may be wanting

In the glare of success, but *that it higher remains.*

Foolish the man who seeks to scorn the natural
pleasures,

Holding glory a dream, love a delusion and snare;

Friendship, too costly a thing for prudent men to
invest in ;

Woman's affection, a ware that can be purchased at
will.

XVI.

When wine sparkles in glass, and your neighbour is
specially charming,

Launching sparks from the eye, that in the fancy
remain,

Happy the moments will pass ; but, sure as the sun of
to-morrow

Rises, reaction will come—pain of the head or the
heart.

Shall we, then, fly from the halls where Bacchus the
rosy is worshipped,

Or where the Paphian Queen kindles the flame of
desire ?

No ! for 'tis better to smart than to pine in a
mouldering cloister,

Where no wine-cup invites, nor the sweet lips of the
fair.

XVII.

Greatest of Nature's gifts, to enjoy and reflect on
  enjoyment,
Climb some steps of the stair to the ideal that leads,
Leaving below the mists that cloud the valley of effort,
Clearer feeling the air wafted from mountain of Truth.

XVIII.

Death is the shadow of life, but shadows wait upon
  sunshine;
Why, if we bask in the one, shall we the other decry?
Each forms part of a plan which gives to mortals
  endeavour,
Will, and passions, and then limits the term of their
  sway.
Travel the wise man enjoys, but, viewing the end of
  his journey,
Calmly the moment awaits under the hill to repose.

XIX.

" Passions I fully control and strive for virtuous action."
Softly, my friend, let me ask, what there is left to
  control?

Are not these troublesome guests in youth and
    vigorous manhood

Buried 'neath hill-slope of time, wept by the tears
    of our age ?

XX.

Shrewd politicians we are and follow the beck of our
    leader,

Cheering all that he says, even his meaningless words.

Have you not seen in the field how one sheep follows
    its fellow ?

Nor does the hindmost enquire whither its comrade
    has gone.

XXI.

" *Now*, my son," said a father, "you enter on life and
    temptation ;

Great are the snares of the world ; difficult 'tis to
    walk straight.

If you walk crooked, remember that serpentine paths
    are the longest,

And often lead at the end into a fathomless pit."

" Governor," answered the youth, " the serpentine path
     is the nicest,
Bordered by fruit and by flow'rs, risking the pit at the
     end."

XXII.

Happy the young who stand on radiant slope of the
     Future,
Hearing murmur of waves rise from the ocean
     of life;
Happy the old who feel that sterling work is
     accomplished,
Somewhat done for the mass, who are hereafter to come—
Certain marks affixed above the tide-level of ages;
Statue that claims its place in the Walhalla of Fame.

XXIII.

Happy is he who works and after working reposes,
Thus fulfilling the plan given to man at his birth—
Every year to feel he's reached to a level that's higher.
Nearer scenting the breeze blowing from hill-top of
     Fame.

XXIV.

Strong is the will that moulds society after its
    likeness,

For 'tis of many made up, that which the public
    we call ;

Here is the test of strength when one man thinks
    for the masses,

Seeing farther than all what are the objects they
    seek.

XXV.

Seek not prizes to win whilst shirking labour and
    effort,

Which our nature exacts, ere we approach to the
    goal.

Some creep softly along, 'mid shade and verdure
    reposing ;

Stained with dust are some, panting in sight of the
    goal.

Near the first may approach, but ne'er can enter the
    temple,

For their limbs, though fresh, cannot be speedy at will.

XXVI.

Wide as the circle may seem of passion, will, and
    endeavour,
When we in youth survey all the horizon of
    life:
Older, the space contracts with each ripe year that is
    passing,
Till there remains at the last only a couch and a
    grave.

XXVII.

When the great Alexander returned from Indian
    conquest:
On deep problems of life, eager with Brachmans
    he spoke;
Questions were answered, and then onward went each
    on his mission,—
One to conquer and die far from his kindred and
    home;
Calmly the others to seek, by thought and deep
    meditation,

What of Man's future may be pictured in destiny's
glass.

When the conqueror died, his empire split into
fragments ;

What the Philosophers taught, lives after ages have
passed.

PART II.

COMPOSITIONS IN RHYMED METRES.

PART II.

COMPOSITIONS IN RHYMED METRES.

EXCURSIONS IN THE PAST.

"Nor centuries have fragments left in vain."

'TWIXT wakefulness and dreams, the mind,
    Poised o'er the shifting sphere of thought,
Of the world's history may find
    The pictures to one centre brought.

Beyond the main and further strand,
    Quick thought has fresh horizons made:
In those far distant climes where stand
    Cedar and palm with grateful shade.

It marks the point in history
    When man his social life begun,

In nomad tribes, with footsteps free,
  Adored the fertilizing sun.

Near to the flood of rolling Nile,
  Myriads of arms vast structures raise :
Temple and tomb, with lofty pile,
  That still attract the wand'rers' gaze.

In naked outline, lone and grand,
  Preaching of glory passed away,
The Pyramids on plain of sand
  Link ancient Egypt with to-day.

Later we pause at Babylon,
  Its temple by fair maidens sought,
Where strangers flocked and looked upon
  Strange images in sculpture wrought.

The Sage, of earthly wisdom tired,
  Learnt of the stars the paths to trace,
And thus with lofty hopes aspired
  To fill all Nature's vacant space.

We see the writing on the wall
    That smote the Monarch's soul with dread,
When fear crept through the festal hall
    And Hebrew Seer his message said.

We gaze upon the Grecian King,
    Entering where Fate its victim calls,—
Term of victorious wandering,
    As death-lights gleam through banquet halls.

Of Greece we see the courtezan
    In snake-like arms her lovers fold ;
By chains of sense enslaving man
    With locks of ebon or of gold.

E'en while those vapours cloud the air,
    Triumphs of intellect we find,
Art lavishes creation fair,
    Philosophy dissects the mind.

Like brightest star in firmament,
    Like words of flame on mystic scroll,

Was Athens on her mission sent,
  Mistress of all that stirs the soul.

Art, eloquence, philosophy,
  And poet's song, and warrior's might,
Blending their varied tints we see,
  And beaming long ere quenched in night.

The early Roman annals give
  Records of high and noble deeds:
One for his land will captive live,
  To save its fame another bleeds.

Later we find a conqueror
  Marching with victory's flag unfurled;
Statesman, surpassing warrior,
  Welds in one mass the Roman world.

A man so great that he who slew,
  Won by his act undying fame;
Each as a type, profoundly true,
  Ambition scorched by vengeance' flame.

The serpent form of Egypt's Queen,
   In fatal fascination fair,
Paints the Triumvir's closing scene,
   Who loses life and empire there.

Look on the arena, head o'er head,
   With lions brought from Afric's shore;
Where captives fought, where martyrs bled
   Till sated people cried, " No more."

     *   *   *   *

Rome falls ; but on the Eastern shore
   Another splendid city stands,—
Byzantium gives to learning more,
   To glory less, in distant lands.

Some rule by thought and some by arms,
   But Mecca's Prophet both combined,—
No danger daunts, no fear alarms
   Moslem of fierce fanatic mind.

Islam rolled onwards like a flood,
　　Engulphing far and wide-spread lands,
And though the West its might withstood,
　　Down to our days its fabric stands.

Then, after centuries of storm,
　　Which countless ruins left behind,
Art lifts again her radiant form,
　　And claims the homage of mankind.

The Imperial City, crowned again,
　　Exacts obedience from the world ;
On Papal edicts rests the stain
　　Of pride at Kings and rulers hurled.

Fouler than deeds of Pagan Prince,
　　The fires that Christian bigots make,
As tortured heretics shall wince,
　　When bound to orthodoxy's stake.

Look where the hosts of chivalry
　　Break like a wave on Paynim shore,

Their leaders great to dare or die,
    When Kings Crusaders' banners bore.

We see, and brighter is the view,
    In Art and eloquence' domain,
Man, to his higher mission true,
    Ruling by intellect again.

Whilst vassals crouch beneath the shade
    Of feudal fortress' giant size,
O'er western seas the passage made,
    Revealed new lands to wondering eyes.

Great legacy for future times,
    For countless myriads ample space :
Nature, in all her varied climes,
    Invites the teeming human race.

      *   *   *   *

And so, 'mid wars and faction's clash,
    We come at last to modern days ;

Feudality, with mighty crash,
　　Sank in a revolution's blaze.

We see the giant arm of steam,
　　And signals flashing through the night,
Tracing in fancy's magic dream,
　　A vast mosaic's pattern bright.

＊　　　　＊　　　　＊　　　　＊

So, when the mind has traversed all
　　The ages of past history,
It wakes to bow at duty's call
　　And work as those who nothing see

Beyond each day's allotted task,
　　Which binds us oft unwilling here ;
So occupied we scarce can ask
　　Why others smile or hide a tear.

And this is best, for if the rein
　　Be loosed on fancy's wingèd steed,

Scant energies for work remain,
   Or discipline for time of need.

And so, at last, illusions fall—
   Dreams are gone by—'tis time to act ;
Vainly we seek to grasp the All,
   And Fancy bows her head to Fact.

DEATH POEMS.

I.

Ah! yes, my friends, the time is short—
  The shadows lengthen on the hill,
And words that we exchanged in sport
  May prove the truest wisdom still.

Life's stream, that bubbles on its course,
  Shall turn aside from ev'ry eye,
And, spent its onward gushing force,
  Leave but a bed with gravel dry.

'Tis sad to wait, 'mid lingering pain,
  The moment of a last farewell,—
To hear the snapping of Time's chain,
  And gloomy waters' mournful swell.

Saddest when clouds of deep regret
  Envelope the last hours of life;

And, vainly striving to forget,
  The mind recalls fierce Passion's strife ;

When Evil's ensign was displayed,
  And Virtue's temple lost to view,
The turning point where choice was made,
  And the false triumphed o'er the true.

The force that bounteous Nature gave,
  Lavished on brief excitement's day ;
No hand the vessel's course to save,
  That floats,—dismasted wreck,—away.

That moment, in its morbid power,
  Honour and right alike forgot.
Tinges with gloom the parting hour,
  In mem'ry's vale the darkest spot.

II.

'TIS well to die 'midst friends ; perhaps
    Some soothing word may then be said,
Some happy scene recalled, that wraps
    The present in the light that's fled.

And yet how little can be done
    By those who ministering stand :
Man leaves for aye life's cheerful sun—
    He sees through mists a shadowy land.

Nor can the formulas of creeds
    True solace to the mind convey ;
In that last hour the spirit needs
    Assurance of a brighter day.

Some sentiment of the Divine—
    Ethereal presence girt with light,
As round our wandering footsteps shine
    The starry glories of the night.

Yet creeds may inner wisdom hide,
    As husks enclose a precious fruit,—
Instincts of goodness that abide,
    And with eternal justice suit.

The warm routine of life that throws
    It's network round the circling day ;
The table's cheer, the fire that glows,
    The room for work, the hall for play—

The family and friends, who weave
    That web through which affection's light
So mildly beams,—*all* must we leave ?
    And varying Nature's aspects bright?

All this, we know, must one day fade.
    But how do men the prospect view ?
The greater part, their life-path made,
    The busy tasks of Time pursue.

Others in pleasure's maze will stray,
    And walking by the senses' light,

Postpone the thought, as best they may,
　　Of the still grave's unwelcome sight.

And some, with higher aims, may think
　　On Hope and Freedom's longed-for day ;
And, standing on the Future's brink,
　　Be warmed by glory's parting ray.

But few, the universal scheme
　　Of Nature to be best allow.
As all must die, why should it seem
　　So hard to tread the pathway now ?

If you are happy and enjoy
　　The vig'rous spring of constant health,
How many victims cares annoy,
　　How close does misery dwell to wealth !

How sharply can the Passions sting.
　　Ambition's fall, the dread recoil
When foiled is energy's last spring
　　And blighted lie the fruits of toil !

What, shall we hesitate to go
   Where all that strove have gone before ?
The Sage, the Hero's plume of snow,
   Greet guests on Pluto's distant shore.

The Captains of the ancient days,
   The high Philosophers who taught
Truth to explore 'mid error's maze,
   And knowledge by experience bought.

Would you prefer at Club to dine,
   Listen to scandal with cigar,
See beauty's eyes with lustre shine
   At festal board the brightest star ?

Why not confess the truth, how few
   Have shaken off the chains of sense,
Or Passion's welcome calls subdue,
   For distant Future's cold suspense !

TO HEALTH.

" Mens sana in Corpore sano."

HALF mistress and half wife,
  Thou cheerest mortal life
    With balmy breath :
We force for action feel,
Though Time, with rolling wheel,
  Lead on to death.

When Pleasure's banner flies,
Flaunting 'gainst cloudless skies
  In brightest hues,
Thy presence gives us force
To bound along the course,
  In path we choose.

Decision's plan is laid
Ere bloom of action fade—

Inspired by thee,
Firm nerves the choice will make,
For higher motive's sake,
    With judgment free.

A healthy nature flies
From meaner thoughts that rise,
    Upheaving life :
Hot passions that destroy,
Cares that disturb our joy
    With ceaseless strife.

In noble action, then,—
Whate'er the choicest men
    Chiefly pursue,—
If excellence you seek,
Preserve the blooming cheek,
    Possessed by few.

Look, maiden, in the glass,
As groups of dancers pass

At crowded ball ;
Let Beauty seek her bed
Ere the last light has fled
From festal hall.

Too anxious man of care !
A few brief moments spare
    From business' hour ;
Take in the park a ride,
Or sit by woman's side,
    Owning her power.

At banquet, when you sit
'Twixt loveliness and wit,
    At pleasure's call :
When flowers glow with light,
And bubbling wines look bright,
    Don't drink of all.

At midnight hour, when smoke
And tale of scandal spoke

Float through the brain :
When ice-cooled drinks are near,
In tall glass foaming clear,
    Learn to refrain.

Then fresh at morning rise,
And feel like bird that flies
    On steadfast wing ;
To occupation's sway
Give what the circling day
    Of force may bring.

On afternoon so clear,
When shouting voices near
    The odds proclaim,
Seek not to make a book,
But in your conscience look,
    Not without shame—

Twelve hundred yesterday,—
A thousand more to pay

On Monday next ;
Life, choicest gift of all,
No spendthrift can recall,
By torments vexed.

Fly from that fair one's smile,
That seems so free from guile,—
'Twill cost you more,
In happiness and health,
Than all the hoarded wealth
In miser's store.

Vision of health ! may'st thou,
With calm and stainless brow,—
Hov'ring in air
Where purest sea-breeze blows,
Or stream through valley flows,—
Our life-plan share.

So, in the later days,
Shall thousand voices raise

A shout sublime :
Each workman's dwelling clean—
No selfish vices seen
    In prosp'rous time.

Health, happiness, shall dwell
Free from the turbid swell
    Of passion's tide ;
No wars shall vex the world,
But conquest's flag be furled,
    And truth abide.

The fight will then be won ;
And, 'neath a mellow sun—
    Evil expelled—
The good shall reign supreme,
And real be Fancy's dream
    Of hopes long held.

FIRST AND LAST KISS.

A BASHFUL youth rushed in to tell
  Of accident that late befel.
    The lady sat alone
In boudoir closed by painted blind ;
She hears his tale, and accents kind
    Murmur in softest tone.

The tale is told, yet still they sit ;
But 'tis not flashing spark of wit
    That chains him to the spot :
His hand meets hers, a glance is given,
A shock through every nerve is driven,
    That ne'er can be forgot.

And as that lovely lady speaks,
New-born desire has flushed his cheeks,

Brought near to beauty's charm ;
Entranced by all experience knows,
His heart beats fast—his being glows
    'Neath tresses soft and warm.

First page of book.that's writ in flame,
Where Passion oft inscribed a name,
    That mounts on Mem'ry's wing !
Recalling many a blissful hour,
When senses owned the magic power
    That beauty's treasures bring.

     *   *   *   *

Life runs its course, and forty years,
With mingled flood of hopes and fears,
    Have sped their onward flight.
Age has approached—ambition's prize
Pursued and won; and women's eyes
    Have beamed with glances bright.

In study, as he sits one day,
An artless girl comes in to say
    Her mother wants a book.
He takes the volume from a shelf,
And, scarcely master of himself,
    He meets her kindly look.

Sweet innocence blooms in her smile ;
That slender form must wait awhile,
    Ere woman's charms appear ;
Sweet lips and pearl-white teeth he sees ;
A kiss is given—the maiden flees
    Like some affrighted deer.

" Ah, ne'er again ! " he sadly cries,
" As Time in destined circle flies ;
    For me these joys are past ;
Yet softer memories may live,
And friendship lasting solace give,
    Though I have kissed my last."

"THE FRAGRANT DUST OF HISTORY."

WHERE blooms the deathless? Say, oh where?
   If not in deeds that yet bear sway,
Whose giant forms yet fill the air,
   'Midst all the interests of to-day?

The graves where Athens' warriors lie
   The pass where Sparta's heroes fell—
Bring tears unbidden to the eye,
   As youths on history's records dwell.

Oh! that those feelings could come back,
   When first we sat in garden's shade,
Exploring Time's illumined track,
   Of Greek and Roman fragments made.

Is it the glory that accrues
   From deeds above the common range?

A mighty presence that subdues
    Minds filled with thoughts that know no change ?

Or is it that we love to dwell
    On actions proving man can soar,
From lower instincts' seething hell,
    To thoughts that bloom for evermore ?

A great example *there* is given,
    Flattering, in truth, to human pride :
Our dusty world seemes linked to heaven,
    And weaker forms in strength abide.

O'er trivial incidents of life
    A light is flashing through the air :
And stirrings of a mighty strife—
    Ideal with the real—are there.

But what to us ideal seems
    Was once enacted on the stage
Of busy life : those brilliant dreams
    Were history to a former age.

Scan, then, the page of mighty deeds,
   O, youthful reader ! till thy mind
Throbs with the great—for anguish bleeds—
   And sympathy with both can find.

And some who, after manhood's course,
   Approach the boundary of their age,
May colour their decaying force
   With hues from history's brightest page.

THE SYREN'S INVITATION.

IN a well-balanced nature, if sensual temptations be
yielded to, their indulgence will be followed by a
reaction, at once physical and moral, into a bracing
atmosphere of thought and action.

See where the flag of pleasure waves,
   And Syren's voice is gently heard,
Inviting to the hidden caves,
   By no intruding tempest stirred.

There chambers gleam with softest light;
   On couches' slope fair forms recline;
Lips parted show their treasures bright,
   And eyes with passion's glances shine.

Here, innocence, that hardly knows
   How near the torrent's brink it stands;

And *there*, matured experience glows,
   When touched by sympathetic hands !

Here is the senses' temple, where
   Tradition's glowing pleasures dwell—
Perfumes float idly through the air,
   With distant music's softened swell.

From old historic lands we find
   Hetairæ with their blandest smile ;
By fancy's dream enthralled, the mind
   Forgets its sorrows for awhile ;

And roseate drapery veils from view
   Half of what mirror's planes repeat ;
Rough satyrs tender nymphs pursue ;
   In forest-glade fond lovers meet.

When love voluptuous forms displays,
   Nor rest nor food its votaries take ;
Objects are seen through fancy's haze,
   With kisses warm the heart-strings quake.

But when desire can throb no more,
   And hours that moments seem are past,
The banquet-hall shall force restore,
   Till night repose may give at last.

We sip thy foaming cup, Champagne ;
   Thy aromatic juice, Bordeaux ;
The golden grape of sunny Spain,
   Or Rhineland's autumn's parting glow.

Yet not too oft ; for Mocha now
   With fragrance o'er the senses steals ;
Restorer of the care-worn brow,
   Or frame that pleasure's languor feels !

And then intelligence comes back
   From voyage to fair Cythera's shore,
It mounts to science' star-lit track,
   And lists to wisdom's voice once more.

In finer nature's balanced frame,
   Beauty and wine may oft beguile

The senses with their vivid flame,
    Yet charm them only for *awhile.*

The mind its equilibrium seeks,
    And freedom claims from pleasure's chain ;
Our higher nature, rising, breaks
    Those rosy bonds—yet turns again,

To look once more on vistas bright,
    Judging their weakness and their strength,—
We analyze enjoyment's light,—
    Are masters of our souls at length.

PARIS:

PERSONAL RECOLLECTIONS.

DEDICATED TO MY ESTEEMED FRIEND,
WILLIAM MEDOWS, ESQ.

WHEN first I Paris saw, youth's cheerful sun
　　Shone on my path with never-ceasing ray ; (1836)
Each morn I woke well braced for work or fun,
　　And quaffed the bowl whose juice Time bears away.

Oh ! ·then I revelled in digestion's power,
　　That bore me onward o'er life's furrowed track ;
Pausing awhile, in Fancy's rose-girt bower,
　　And happier still, perchance, when looking back.

Years had flowed on : in manhood's prime I came,
　　And love and friendship smiled on either hand ;　.
Paris was scorched by Revolution's flame,
　　And faction's rage had blazed o'er Gallia's land.
　　　　　　　　　　　　　　　　(1848-50)

'Twas then I read and mused ;—the world, a book
  Whose page each day some fresh experience brought ;
Mere pleasure's path my mind had long forsook,
  But glory's rays in studious hours were sought.

A Ruler came, and awed the masses, till
  Paris in newest splendour stood arrayed : (1853-62)
Long lines of palaces kept rising still—
  Delighted tourists roamed by stream and shade.*

Happy I was, sipping the glorious wine,
  Poured, by experience, in life's mantling cup ;
If then less brightly youth's illusions shine,
  We feel a steady power that bears us up ;

Bears us aloft o'er every mean desire,
  And lets us cull of life the choicest flower :
For youth's first years, with intermittent fire,
  Oft strand us at the close of Passion's hour.

---

* In the renovated Bois de Boulogne.

Each Spring I came and blessed the city where
    So much enjoyment to my portion fell ;
Of literature I scanned the records fair—
    Pages, where fancy and instruction dwell.

Two horses bore me round the smiling Bois, –
    Mute friends, whose portraits daily* I survey,—
Glimpses of many-coloured life I saw,
    Whose hues still wear the freshness of to-day.

And once again, when throughout Europe rung (1867)
    A call to pilgrims from each distant land,
To fairer shrine than ever poet sung,
    Treasures of art and skill on either hand,

With deep delight I viewed that magic scene,
    Of human skill the panorama fair ;
All had sprung up, where late a plain had been
    Of arid sand, a desert nude and bare.

---

* Now in my dining-room.

Say, shall I come once more, when age his seal
    Has stamped on pond'rous frame and footstep slow?
Can Paris still some former joy reveal ?
    Does Friendship call me with its roseate glow ?

Yes ; one is there whom I would gladly meet,
    In friendly converse o'er thy juice, Bordeaux.
On dusty plain of life his voice I'd greet,
    And think on pleasure's dream of years ago !

POSTSCRIPTUM, DECEMBER, 1870.

Since this was writ, what awful change has come,
    What cloud of woe broods o'er that city fair !
Beleaguering hosts are there with beat of drum,
    And shells bear swift destruction through the air.

Yet, crown of glory rests on Paris still,
    Brighter than when of sportive pleasures Queen ;
Greater she stands on self-denial's hill,
    And myriad patriots grace the solemn scene.

No more the dance, with its enthralling power,
　　Or music's strains in lamp-lit halls by night,
Make Time half loath to seize the passing hour,—
　　Each moment now is destined to the fight.

That fight for Freedom on which glory's rays
　　So oft misnamed, shall now resplendent fall ;
Victors or vanquished share its sacred blaze,
　　For rightful cause when Man devotes his all.

SOLITUDE.

Y ON elder sits in gilded room alone,
    Silence unbroken by familiar tone—
His eye falls listlessly on vacant space,
-And pleasure veils her half-averted face.
Thick falls the rain, wild blows the wind *without*,
Within, no youthful voices joyous shout—
All is for one combined; the master's will
Finds in attendants' zeal its echo still.
No free spontaneous glow of life is there,
No light that crosses the dark path of care—
His thoughts, concentred, trace their circling flight,
But none react against the gloom of night.
Neat folded journals on the table lie;
And newest fiction, with spasmodic cry
Of passion, working through the social maze—
Travels in varied climes, and Art displays
The gracious outlines, with suggestive skill,

Which memory may with glowing colours fill.
In vain they call,—no friendly voice is there,
Nor sympathetic glance, that foe to care.
Alone he lives, and finds, through each dull year
Ennui's black spectre ever drawing near.
No friendly converse, where wit bears its part,
Or free discussion limits gives to art.
Firmly it grasps its prey—all hope seems fled,
And man, still living, dwells but with the dead.

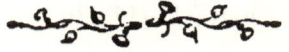

FAME.

VISION of glory ! Through long ages past
    Enthroned in light :
Artist or bard, on whom thy rays were cast,
    Rejoiced in might.

Creative power was felt : the song was sung
    To golden lyre ;
From marble's block the god-like features sprung,
    Instinct with fire.

The warrior led his hosts across the earth,
    Glory to gain ;
And thousands died to aid that stormy birth,
    Or writhed in pain.

The orator entranced his hearers' breast
    And ruled their will,
They fed upon his words with eager zest,—
    Envy was still.

Fame's craving yet subsists in many a mind
        Alone that dwells ;
Life's occupations vainly seek to bind
        The heart that swells.

That banner, with seductive colours wrought,
        Flutters in view ;
And Fancy's vision, through long vigils sought,
        Obscures the true.

All would they give for Fame : the tranquil rest
        Of peaceful days,
Love, friendship—every charm their lot has blest
        For Glory's blaze.

But few can win ; to many comes the day
        Of bitter grief ;
Too late they feel how they have cast away
        Of goods the chief.

Friends slighted come not back ; the love that's dead
        Blooms not again ;

Health's balmy breath no more on life is shed—
    Days pass in pain.

Yet Fame there is on nobler acts that rests,
    Found when least sought :
Endeavour scales yon mountain's highest crests,
    By labour bought ;

Then anchors in a bay, serene and bright,
    Life's vessel fast :
Love, friendship, honour, ever kept in sight,
    With calm at last.

DESPONDENCY.

CLOUDS veil at times our being's brilliant sun
      With black unrest;
We feel, e'er half life's vigorous course is run,
      Dimly oppressed.

Thought from its highest flight at once will fall,
      With weary wing :
Indifferent we feel well nigh to all
      Fortune may bring.

Shall this be ever so ?   To most there comes
      Returning light.
And Nature's equilibrium, that sums
      Repose of night.

Yet not to all ; some minds sink deeper down,
      As each year rolls,

And Nature's face wears an eternal frown
　　To troubled souls.

Too deeply lost they seem in error's maze,
　　Again to rise ;
Misfortune's clouds, through lapse of gloomy days,
　　Give no bright skies.

Say, on our bark shall hope her welcome sail
　　No longer raise—
To bear us far beyond the tempest's wail
　　To tranquil bays ?

Shall ever in our ears the echo ring
　　Of boding voice ;
And not one single hour recall the spring
　　When hearts rejoice ?

Error of vision, the half-broken glass
　　Of mis-spent life,
Gives back distorted images, that pass
　　In cloudy strife.

Real they are not.   O man, thy complex fate
    Bright suns again
May welcome, if endeavour, not too late,
    Struggle with pain.

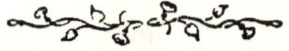

SATIETY.

A SHADOW comes, bright Summer's day that veils
    And clouds its sky ;
Then flap of life's proud bark the slackened sails,
    And drooping lie.

A feeling comes that kindred claims to pain,
    As Time's waves roll ;
Its fetters seem the links of endless chain
    Binding the soul.

What brooding image makes swift action pause
    In listless calm ?
Say, in obedience to what secret laws
    Lost is life's balm ?

What wound corrodes the mind as it surveys
    A misspent past ?

Anticipating dull and pain-fraught days,
    With gloom o'ercast?

It is Satiety,—the monstrous brood
    Of sorceress,
Erect like serpent with its crested hood
    And foul caress.

Naught bright or lovely meets the eye again
    In all this world;
A numbness comes, more hard to bear than pain,
    'Gainst Nature hurled.

List not to promptings of the evil mind,
    Unhappy man;
Nor better instincts by excitement blind;—
    Work while you can.

Pleasures may fail to charm; it is their law;
    Yet strive for good:
Such efforts once a happier prospect saw,
    When understood.

False visions disappear; the victor's palm
    May yet be gained;
On Virtue's mount dwells an eternal calm,
    By storm unstained.

Start, then, your task to meet; *now* sounds the hour,—
    Now breaks the day;
Soon will those demon forms regain their power,
    If you delay!

PASTORAL, TO CLARA.

OH, Clara! the day shall be yours: and I feel
    So entranced with delight,
That a century's life could not fully reveal
    All that beams on my sight.

See, the " trotters " are come to the door, and we'll go
    To the shore of the lake;
And the chariot of Phœbus would seem but too slow
    Our bright journey to make.

Oh ! how lovely you look in that dress ; and your eyes
    Give a promise to-day
That no cloud on the sky of your heart shall arise,
    As together we stray.

And the déjeuner's packed in the hamper, with ice,
    Just to cool the champagne ;
When I fill up your glass, will you murmur " How nice !"
    Nor my service disdain ?

But a year has elapsed since you dawned on the world
    With your conquering smile ;
And three months since our bridal joy's banner unfurled
    In Cythera's bright isle.

Blooming flowers, in the vases, shall greet our return,
    In mute homage to you ;
And the lamp, with an exquisite odour, shall burn,
    As our home we review.

And the chamber, where love lies asleep in each fold
    Of the curtains you chose ;
Where the mirror gave back, from its framework of gold,
    Your fair form as you rose.

Mount quickly ! for, see, how impatient the steeds
    Paw the ground, till they seem
Like runners who succour a victim who bleeds
    By some carnage-stained stream.

Most charming of days, blessed with finest of skies,
    Will be ours for the trip ;

And I gaze on the kindest and brightest of eyes,
    And the loveliest lip.

We are off! And the scene looks too fair to be true;—
    Yet it is so, I know:
For I feel a soft breeze wafting kisses to you,
    As triumphant we go.

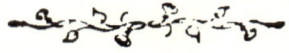

WOMAN'S ADORATION.

YES; she adored him, if that term be given
 To feelings that on high an altar raise,
With longings that in vain for good had striven,
 Concentred now with bright but fatal blaze,

On a poor mortal's heart, unworthy oft
 E'en the reflection of such light to know;
Hard selfish nature grinding down the soft,—
 Double deception sure to end in woe:

First to the victim who so blindly trusts,
 Then to the man whom flatterers ever spoil.
Till from his breast all higher aims he thrusts,
 Smiling on slaves who for his pleasures toil.

Bathed in the vapours of cœrulean space,
 Or tinged with purple of the coming storm,
High thoughts each other through her being chase,
 Ere they subside and settle into form;

Resulting in a woman's fervent love,
  Which to ideal realms aspires in flight,
Seeking a soul all meaner thoughts above,
  Draped in the mantle of heroic might.

By all the anguish of high hopes deceived,
  The dread recoil, when Fancy's bubbles burst,
We estimate how full that heart believed,—
  How vast the rainbow arch it spanned at first !

SOLITUDE AND SOCIETY.

LE POUR ET LE CONTRE.

I.

A YE, shut the door, I'll not be bored,—
   I've bid the world a long farewell ;
What can society afford
   To one its shams who knows so well !

I know it all by heart : they sit
   With formal look at banquet fair ;
We've waited long for social wit,
   And find but feeble echo's there.

Well do I know the morning call,
   The afternoon with crowded " Drum,"
The listless look that sits on all
   Who from routine to visit come ;

The Club, where languid loungers yawn,
    Draining of wine the frequent glass,
And, careless of the future, pawn
    Their health, that all too soon will pass;

The promenade, where still you meet
    Faces that bear thy brand, Ennui,
The aimless tread of many feet,
    With effort occupied to be.

When nought the dull horizon breaks,
    When nothing that we hear or see
A rippling wave of interest wakes
    Or sets imagination free.

I know the wares in ev'ry shop;
    The girl that from the counter smiles;
Each evening comes that elder fop,
    Chasing his game with cunning wiles.

I watch the waves as one by one
    They break upon the pebbly shore,—

I envy those whose work is done,
   Till sunlight calls to toil once more.

Close, then, my door, I'll live alone !
   Live on remembrance of the past—
Its colours on Time's threshold thrown,
   Like reflex hues on church floor cast.

II.

Shut out the world, my friend ! But *how* ?
   Are you not part of it yourself ?
'Tis hard at Fashion's shrine to bow ;
   Harder to pine on dusty shelf.

'Tis well midst rows of books to sit,
   Scanning of literature the page,—
Too late we find we have not hit
   The mark proposed in earlier age.

You say you know the world by heart,—
   'Tis but that world's machinery ;

Of human minds the inner part
    Leaves much for longest life to see.

Ennui can many aspects wear :
    It haunts the crowds of fashion, true.
But do its vulture talons spare
    Those who a lonely path pursue ?

Can well-filled shelves enjoyment give,
    To match with social circle's claim ;
Where fresh-born feelings breathe and live,
    And youthful bosoms pant for fame ?

Picture and book are precious when
    They symbolize our inward thought,
And aid imagination's ken,
    In topics for discussion brought.

He who is severed from his kind,
    Nor interest in his fellows takes,
To every hope of progress blind,
    Commits the gravest of mistakes.

Proudly concentred, let him dwell
   In life's long avenue alone ;
But would he inward feelings tell,
   He'd speak, perchance, with humbler tone—

Seeking for sympathy, that waves
   Her banner o'er the human race ;
Affection, that from numbness saves,
   And fills with light our life-path's space.

TO VICTOR HUGO.

GREAT Poet, in an age when much is small,
    And action's meted by self-interest's rule—
Great dramatist, evoking at his call
    Indignant protests 'gainst corruption's school.

An orator, whose voice with restless might,
    Against oppression's sway o'er act or thought,
Pleaded for nations' or for classes' right,
    In accents not to be coerced or bought.

Artist of highest aim and genial powers,
    Whether with mediæval life he deals,
And passion's struggles round the time-worn towers,*
    Or of our modern days the purport feels.

With gen'rous instincts ever on the wing,
    Apostle of a brighter future's day—

---

* Notre Dame de Paris.

When ev'ry worker's toil reward shall bring,
   When Freedom owns no laws' unequal sway.

His magic pen oft by a word conveys
   Some vivid outline ne'er to be forgot :
The courtezan her new-born life pourtrays,
   And true affection heals corruption's blot.*

When human adoration rises till
   A power divine alone its aims express,—
With fine gradations the Eternal Will
   Bends down from Heaven a mortal love to bless.†

When, in December's day, so bright and cold,
   All Paris thronged to see the ashes brought
Of him whose name was wreathed with glory's fold,
   The Poet's voice expressed the general thought.‡

---

* Marion de l'Orme.
         "l'amour a refait ma virginité."

† "Enfant, si j'etais Dieu."
         (Rayons et Ombres.)—December, 1840.

‡ "Le jour fut rayonnant comme ta gloire,
        Et froid, comme ton tombeau !"

And from the tribune when his accents fell,
　All Europe caught the spark that burst in flame;
Such fiery words 'gainst all who Freedom sell,
　Such withering scorn for slaves to Order's name.

　　　　　　　　　　　　　　(1849-51.)

Finer the lesson, when he tells us how
　Man may be rescued from the depths of crime;
When laws before the great hereafter bow,
　And penal fetters fall in riper time.

　　　　　　　　　　　　("Les Miserables.")

Wrapt in the mantle of poetic fire,
　From rocky isle he looked with eagle's glance,
Till Paris called in need for him whose lyre
　Immortal glory gave to modern France.

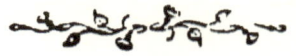

EXILED FROM HOME;

OR, THE LIQUIDATION OF A LIMITED LIABILITY COMPANY.

WE leave the home, where love has smiled,
    Where friendship's manly hand was pressed,
Where song has oft the hours beguiled,
    And wit to converse gave its zest;

Where dinner's genial hour has called
    To table spread with choicest fare,
And genii of the grape enthralled
    The chosen guests assembled there;

The library whose shelves were filled
    With ancient and with modern lore,
And poesy its balm distilled
    In lines that live for evermore;

The bed where often we reclined,
    And, severed from the cares of earth,
'Twixt wakefulness and rest, the mind
    Rose upwards to a higher birth.

'Twas in this house our fate allowed
    A genial span of middle life ;
E'er yet by age the frame was bowed,
    But free from youthful passion's strife,

Too credulous we heard the tale
    Of sleek projector with his lies,
Of Companies that could not fail
    To share in fortune's golden prize.

" Twenty per cent. of dividend,
    " A bonus, too, you're sure to find ;
" For thousand shares, then, promptly send.''
    We bought them all, to prudence blind.

And now the liquidator's call
    Has swallowed up our cherished store ;

We leave our home, our friends, and all
 The flowers that bloomed on life's bleak shore.

We travel, not, as in the days
 When joyful planning our return;
But grope through disappointment's haze
 Where friendship's lights but dimly burn.

INTRO-SPECTION.

L INK of the passions that binds
　　Man to his destiny here;
Glitter of glory that blinds
　　Mortals to sorrow and fear;

Glimpses of radiant beam,
　　Visions of artist or bard,
Plunged in Reality's stream,
　　Turn to the common and hard.

All that embellishes life;
　　All that Fame's visions can show;
Cut by Adversity's knife,
　　Leave but their fragments below.

As from a mountain, the sage,
　　Gazing on valley and rill,

Sees, at the close of his age,
  Shadows that wander at will—

So, if on confines of night
  Feeling and thought we would weigh,
One is too subtle for sight;
  Fast fleets the other away.

What, then, remains to be told?
  Where is the residue left?
Only when feeling is cold
  Are we of Hope's star bereft.

RESPICE FINEM.

L ONG had he roved where'er caprice had led,
　　Long had he sunned himself in Fancy's light,
By streams from that eternal ocean fed
　　Which glitters ever fair to mortal sight.

And then came o'er him, what befalls us all,
　　A certain relaxation of the spring
Which moves our will with energetic call,
　　And gives the reign to fair imagining.

Few see the change Time works in elder days,
　　And fewer still know when to pause and think ;
Withdrawing somewhat with a cautious gaze,
　　Ere they approach the Future's shelving brink.

For hard it is to recognize the fact,
　　That we are sinking down whilst others rise ;
And harder still, with purpose firm to act,
　　Turning our glance from wealth or pleasure's prize.

VALE.

HE'S gone : the bard, whose patriot lyre,
  With far-resounding string,
Awakened souls with words of fire,
  That solemn mem'ries bring.

Nor charmed us less with accents low,
  Pleading for pity's claim—
True lovers' interrupted vow,
  Youth's blasted hopes of fame !

His varied works the germs unfold
  Of purpose—motive—will—
Hot passions' shock 'gainst barriers cold,
  A conflict raging still.

In public life he bore a part,
  Consistent—noble—free ;
Some called it politician's art—
  All felt its dignity.

Poet and Orator—in sweet
    Domestic circle bound;
His ready smile would ever greet
    The friends that sat around.

No angry temper's sudden flash
    Disturbed that sky serene;
Nor irritation's ceaseless plash
    Marred the enchanting scene.

He filled a glorious page in life;
    Was happy in his death:
Ere yet, envenomed faction's strife
    Assailed him with its breath.

Crowds flocked around his tomb to bless—
    He's reached the distant shore:
His country holds one patriot *less*,
    One cherished mem'ry *more*.

CONTRASTS.

WE oft for new horizons call,
　　And never pause to think how all
　　　　Vibrates round central plan—
As Time unwinds the mighty chain
Of mingled hope and joy and pain,
　　　　That binds the world to man.

Some are condemned to live alone,
And hear of life the undertone,
　　　　In murmurs from afar;
From action all divorced they feel,
And watch the turning of the wheel
　　　　That moves the social car.

And some so busy are, they find
Gone the elastic spring of mind
　　　　And dulled perception's glass!

No longer able to enjoy,
As cares life's purer gold alloy,
   And gloomy shadows pass !

Experience will tell us how
We best may utilize the Now,
   When, in historic blaze,
All that we dream of high and bright
Is welded by the furnace-light
   Of Wisdom's gathered days.

SPRING.

FINE days of Spring, what bring ye to the heart?
   What thoughts from higher spheres our natures
                      [cross?
In busy feeling's renovated part,
   What shall we count as gain and what as loss?

Restless, we muse, and wand'ring odours, cast
   From ocean's waves, by secret thoughts are stirred.
We dream of travel—of the changeful past:
   Remembrance faintly throbs, like echo heard.

Yes! suns as bright our eyes have seen before;
   Nature was mirrored in as pure a glow;
And Memory points, through Time's half-opened door,
   Where forms we loved so well, as shadows go.

And some are thinking of the *Season's* rush,
   When chariots roll, and eager rivals strive:

Masses of life. that feeble natures crush,
　　Whilst stronger frames at wished-for goal arrive.

Some dream of odds, and of the horse that wins
　　Just by a head, and saves a mighty stake;
Others of love's entrancing hour, that spins,
　　Down flowery slope, to disappointment's lake.

Each has his vision; but, in nearly all,
　　Of self, the mute, gigantic spectre stands;
Few pause to feel humanity's great call,
　　Or aid the struggling with assisting hands.

Yet selfish feelings work for Nature's plan:
　　Each grooves his path, that in broad ways unite;
Society absorbs the complex man,
　　And narrow purpose tends to wider sight.

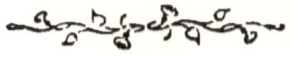

RETROSPECTION.

IT is a solemn moment when, in halls of lonely
    thought,

The ghosts of many a buried year to mem'ry's shrine
    are brought ;

Some glittering with auroral dew beneath the sunny light

Where still a radiant fancy leaves its colours ever
    bright,—

The day when young ambition first has won its school-
    boy prize,

Or first a timid love is met by sympathetic eyes ;

When, with collegians gay, we sat around the festal
    board,

Tasting what mirthful spirits can in youth's gay hours
    afford ;

And when the lines were first composed, half trembling
    as we writ,

Dreaming of poet's laurel crown, the mark our shaft
    must hit ;

And when we travelled through the lands illustrated
by fame,

And felt our bosoms wildly thrill at each historic
name;

And when the marriage bells rang out on summer's
brightest day,

And we beheld the chosen one from rivals borne
away;

And when Election's day came on, 'mid contest close
and keen,—

So popular a candidate had never there been seen,—

'Gainst power, wealth, and influence, a gallant fight
was won,

Heading the poll by ten, 'mid cheers, ere set that
autumn sun.

And later, when, in crowded House, one night we rose
to speak,

And felt our cause was strong, although our voice
seemed somewhat weak,

But unexpected succour came as periods rolled along,

And when we ended cheers arose from that assembled
throng.

Enchanting moment when we see thy radiant form,
  Success,
And 'mid the shouts of victory mankind our worth
  confess :
Bright visions these, and yet the heart confesses, as it
  scans
The vista of our bygone years with all their cherished
  plans,
That sorrow oft has shed o'er joy its dim and misty veil,
And disappointment curled the wave where youth's
  bright vessels sail ;
Yet hope in human breasts still lies like early dew on
  flowers,
Or glances through the breaking clouds as sunshine
  after showers ;
It germs, a tender plant, beneath the bare and rocky
  shade ;
It shines through tears like purest gem amidst the
  waters laid.*

---

* These four lines are paraphrased from the German.

And thus we find in man's career the sombre and the
    bright,

Dark threads of sorrow's web 'mid sparks that kindle
    into light.

Wise is the man who thoughtfully his onward course
    will steer,

And, smiling on the buried past, find e'en sad
    mem'ries dear;

For griefs and failures help to fill for us the final cup,

Wherein Experience is found for ever brimming up.

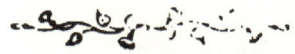

THE MAN OF A THOUSAND.

" Integer vitæ."—Horace.

IN autumn day, when winds their booty bore
    Of fallen leaves,
When garnered was at length the mellow store
    Of golden sheaves :

A man on mossy bank reclined, where fell
    The sun's bright rays,
And memory brought him back the wond'rous spell
    Of bygone days.

He saw his childhood's home—the welcome smile
    That hovered there—
The world's experience, free from craft or guile—
    The evening prayer :

In atmosphere of light and love, where grew
    Youth's blooming flower ;

Whilst glimpses of the outer-world renew
  The passing hour.

Later came glowing manhood's boist'rous sports,
  Perspective bright ;
The chase—long travel to earth's famed resorts,
  Ennobling sight.

For once the retrospect scant record gave
  Of errors past :
So slight it rippled, like a dying wave,
  Calmed down at last.

Well had he kept those years of searching power
  Apart from vice.
While temperance had won health's precious dower
  Of matchless price.

Each year is self-control more easy made
  To thoughtful man ;
And each developed energy will aid
  Life's earnest plan.

Athlete in Virtue's camp, long had he striven
    The fallen to raise,
Whose life temptation's evil power had driven
    To crooked ways.

Faith grew with him, like some wide-spreading tree,
    Whose branches give
Repose to wand'rers, who from tempests flee,
    And learn to live.

Each year brought to his mind maturer power,
    Calm joined to force :
The will that rules despondency's dark hour,
    And turns its course.

He saw of earth the shadows crossed with light,
    Beneath man's feet ;
Beyond, his glance would pierce the sphere of light,
    Where angels greet.

Chaste and abstemious, he had reached the prize
    So seldom gained :

That calm where lower thoughts would blush to rise
In heart unstained.

Active, he could have won the victor's crown
In ages past ;
Swiftest to run or vault, or hold his own
In toils that last.

When from the blush of morn till ev'ning falls
The wand'rer goes
O'er rugged peaks, by glacier's slipp'ry walls,
Through pathless snows,

A rainbow arc of aspirations pure
Links heaven to earth,—
Belief in good conducts by gradients sure,
To higher birth.

And light in vivid coruscations falls
On innocence
That dwells secure in truth's primeval halls,
With purer sense.

*   *   *   *

Roused from the depths of thought, he left the spot
    With rapid pace,
Enthralled by claims that duty's call allot
    To each day's space.

A man esteemed by all : for nobler mind
    Was ne'er allied
To softer feelings—sympathies more kind,
    Unmixed with pride.

PARALLELS.

I.

THE moment ere the fleeting cloud
   Shall bathe itself in light :
Or ocean's wave shall burst its shroud,
   Dissolved in sparkles bright,—

That awful stillness in the air,
   The travail in Earth's womb,
Blasting some land or city fair,
   With swift o'erwhelming doom,—

The point where Nature seems to turn,
   And bare her breast to man,
With quiverings from the mystic urn
   Where sleeps the eternal plan,—

All these are typified in hearts
   On brink of great resolve !
Where restless action's embryo-parts
   In circle dim revolve.

II.

I LOVE to watch the waves of life
  Break on Time's pebbled shore,
Where rises, like the tempest's strife,
  A restless people's roar.

I love the summer's light that falls
  On many a toiling throng,
The bell that stalwart workmen calls
  To bear their load along.

For action has a potent charm
  For those who inly think
How best may reach man's outstretched arm
  To shifting Future's brink.

Yet more I prize the fruitful thought
  From earnest hearts that comes,

With victory by no bloodshed bought,
Marked by no beat of drums.

In the fair Future's golden light,
When Hope her banner waves,
She points to this inscription bright,
And patriots' names engraves.

———————

III.

REMONSTRANCE.

" FATE," the poet cries,
    " Grant my utmost will—
Let my Muse that flies,
    Earth with glory fill."

" Glory," saith the sage,
    " Is a fevered dream ;
Brief its brighter stage,
    Soon obscured its beam."

Many a heart desired
    Such a lot to win ;
But too soon aspired,
    Life's work to begin.

" Yes, I will be great !"
    Rashly swears the youth ;

" And for adverse fate,
    Little cares in truth."

" Sit in patience' school,
    Ere so high you reach—
Cease to play the fool,
    Learn before you teach ! "

Such the counsel wise
    Many a Master gives,
Whilst in youthful eyes
    Naught but glory lives.

Let the Master guide
    Minds that upward soar ;
Counsel sage provide,
    But control no more.

Good it is to see
    Restless soul of youth
Mount on pinion free
    Towards the realm of Truth.

HAS BEEN AND WILL BE.

OFT have we idly dreamed that happiness
    Never again could, as of old, be ours;
That joy no more our troubled sky would bless,
    Or sunshine follow Fate's descending showers.

Error of vision ! in our nature's plan
    Sleep and digestion vital force renew;
What has been circles still round life of man,
    No fatal barrier bounds his shortened view.

The pains of yesterday no longer sting;
    Regrets grow fainter as their objects fade;
Recurrent seasons Nature's offerings bring,
    Light beams anew around the darkest shade.

No jarring discord permanently dwells;
    The ravages of war are healed by peace;

Nature's vast bosom with fresh increase swells ;
Each biting care of life will one day cease.

Why then, O man, thy petty shadow take
To measure forces that around thee play ?
Sorrow and joy their shade and sunshine make
In endless series to the latest day.

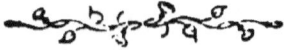

TO A LADY ON HER BIRTHDAY.

TO Lena, on her natal day,
What word of welcome can I say,
What friendly off'ring bring ?
Time 'neath his chariot wheels has cast
Those phantom forms we name the Past,
A half forgotten thing.

And yet this year hath seen the fall
Of throne and empire, fraught with all
The woes that war can give,
As man, ingenious to destroy,
Feels in the crash a fearful joy,
If glory's rays but live.

Rather I'd contemplate a face
Where dwells, with unaffected grace,
A woman's earnest will :
Some lines of thought and feeling there,
Crossed by a smile supremely fair,
Enchain the fancy still.

What tale does the expression tell ?
Is it of mem'ries loved so well,
    Or scenes that once were bright ?
Or is she seeking where to find
A loving, sympathetic mind,
    To bless her eager sight ?

Dear lady, we are wand'rers all,
Our footsteps echo through the hall
    Which life above us rears :
Some, pleasures near their path may see,
But more from sad deceptions flee ;
    And joy oft ends in tears.

Yet, if our wishes could prevail,
We'd ask of fate a fav'ring gale
    To waft thee to the shore,
Where peace and happiness shall dwell,
Far distant from the turbid swell
    Of sorrows felt no more.

SI JEUNESSE SAVAIT—SI VIEILLESSE POUVAIT.

OFT in his waking dreams there came
 A certain semblance of the past :
Dark shadows crossed by tongues of flame,
 Or misty veil o'er sunshine cast.

Forms in their outline incomplete,
 Nor rounded by a workman's hand :
Where false perspective's vistas meet,
 And giant temples rest on sand.

So 'tis at best a partial view
 Of life's great stage that men obtain ;
Around lie fragments of the true,
 And pleasure's light is crossed by pain.

For man's allotted journey lies
 Beyond the valley and the hill ;

And all that meets his eager eyes
　　Is vexed by wand'ring phantoms still.

From passion free, the sage may look
　　On shifting cloud and blue expanse:
Long has he studied Nature's book,
　　Ere such a prospect meets his glance.

He looks, but feels his vigour gone
　　For struggles in the stormy fight;
And every prop he leans upon
　　Bears witness to declining might.

Yet some, in youth's all-conquering hour,
　　The boon of knowledge have obtained;
Keen sight is joined to nervous power,
　　And life's stern victory is gained.

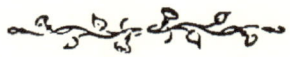

THE SPECTRE.

IT was not in the churchyard's gloom,
  With hurried steps as wanderers pass
Through creaking gate nigh to the tomb,
  Where victims sleep 'mid tangled grass.

Nor in the dark and lonesome dell,
  Where trees up to the pathway stand ;
Of feet when fancied echoes fell,
  And eyes came glaring nigh at hand.

Nor was it in the corridor
  Of lonely dwelling vast and old,
Where awful whispers haunt the floor,
  That make the listener's blood run cold.

Not when, through long-drawn hours of night,
  No moment of repose appears ;

And, straining after morning's light,
    The weakened eyes suffuse with tears,

And shadowy forms are circling where,
    The shaken nerves their vigil keep—
Mephitic vapours float in air,
    Like wavelets on a tideless deep.

That spectre came at festive hour,
    When banquet-hall was filled with light,—
Its shadow crept with numbing power,
    Eclipsing all the tableaux bright.

Remorse, disgust, their fatal screen,
    Before life's lustre interpose ;
No more one ray of pleasure seen,
    As morning's orb returning rose.

Such is the spectre that appals,
    Like pillar on a waste of sand.
Of cheerful guest no footstep falls,
    On vast expanse of blighted land.

And cloudy skies for ever brood
   On murky water's dim expanse;
Despair alone can find its food
   Where beams no more youth's joyous glance.

Can aught avail, of human power,
   Such Spectre from its home to chase?
Yes, if we see, in life's last hour,
   An injured one's forgiving face.

LAST SCENE OF ALL.

TO melancholy instincts true,
   His thoughts maintained their constant flight:
At evening's hour, of sombre hue;
   At morning, with its robe of light.

By meal, that once refreshed, oppressed;
   No more can foaming goblet cheer—
No more, at call of fashion dressed,
   Gay promenaders' groups appear.

Dark solitude its web has wove,
   Through days that even lengthened seem:
The footsteps fall in cypress grove,
   And life seems but a morbid dream.

The leprous scurf of passions dead,
   Flutt'ring desire that rubs its chain,

No crown for age's honoured head,
   No pleasures that untouched remain,—

All these invade the mind by turns,
   Which no ennobling instinct feels,—
It shivers with despair, or burns,
   Or with a last excitement reels.

As Alcohol its whip applies,
   That poison coveted by man,
Through haze when cherished objects rise
   With outline grand and gorgeous plan,

   'Mid phantoms indistinct and vast,
      The force of will that seems like all
   We once possessed in years long past,
      When free from age's numbing thrall ;

   And visions of delight there came,
      As in the days when all was ours,
   Present and future, tinged with flame,
      And glowing in their added powers.

But soon is gone the magic spell ;
    It vanishes ere morning breaks.
Each prostrate nerve has heard its knell,
    Whilst round him coil delirium's snakes.*

Such is the heritage that oft
    One fatal error leaves behind
For those who wildly spring aloft,—
    To steps that lead to greatness, blind.

---

  * One of the most common illusions in the drunkard's delirium
is a vision of serpents coiling round the limbs.

IMPROMPTU *BOUTS RIMÉS.*

I.

CRUSHED under weight of books our epoch *groans*,
  So little matter fills thick volume's *size;*
The wiser mind will speak in under *tones,*
  Whilst shallow thought from thick octavo *cries.*

II.

See where yon flower displays its vivid *bloom,*
  Nor shrinks beforehand from the coming *blast;*
So mortal pleasures, bounded by a *tomb,*
  Mark not the shadow from death's pillar *cast.*

III.

1 will follow if you lead the *way ;*
  For a leader should promptly *advance,*
And a word of encouragement *say*
  To the crowd that depends on his *glance.*
Then lead on with your luminous *eyes,*
  That dispel e'en the darkness of *night,*
And ere Luna in Heaven shall *rise,*
  They will open a fountain of *light.*

IV.

THE OLD BELLE'S LAMENT.

Before me now I see my future *doom*,—
A lonely cottage for my living *tomb*.
In vain for those who once admired I *cry*;
Far from my presence now in haste they *fly*.
No efforts to attract them would I *spare*;
But none, alas! my lonely lot will *share*.
No more they eye me in the crowded *park*;
My charms are gone, and all around is *dark*.

V.

In the world's kitchen seize the widest *pan*,—
Of satire grasp the breeze-compelling *fan*;
Gather life's crumbs into a thrifty *basket*,—
You must succeed; for other rules don't *ask it*.

VI.

Some blame their luck, others the force of *love*,
    As thousands slip away, alas, too *lightly*;
Let circumstances give one adverse *shove*,
    You're done for ever, as you judge most *rightly*.

"CŒLUM NON ANIMAM MUTANT."

IN youth or manhood's prime we leave our home,
  To fix our tent elsewhere with some regret ;
For habit weaves its network round our lives,
Enclosing spheres of darkness mixed with light.
But youth may hope that change will pleasure bring,
Some newer love, or grasp of friendship's hand ;
Some steps in the world's ladder to be climbed—
Some laurel leaf of fame for thought or act.
Too oft deceptive are their hopes ; yet still
They cheer the mind, like the mirage that shows
Fountains or palaces to pilgrim's eye.
To many, life's career will be the same ;
For Fashion, like a thirsty plain of sand,
Absorbs the energies that ever flow
From bubbling fountain of unvaried health,—
Billiards or whist, protracted hours of ball,
When vague excitement struggles with fatigue,
And fevered slumbers bring a vacant day,

To yawn at Club, and drain the frequent glass,—
No healthful breeze of morn o'er Ocean's wave,
Wafting its briny odours from the West ;
Or where the mountain rears its crest sublime,
Like Nature's bulwark o'er a fertile plain.

*   *   *   *

But when, in age, we seek, with pond'rous frame
And weakened mind, that scarce knows how to choose,
Some new abode, elaborate in all
That art or showy comfort can suggest,
What can we hope for, but that black ennui
Shall sit a constant guest by hearth and home,
Through hours that drag their dreary course along,
Whilst mem'ries of the past, of errors such
As mark the turning-point in man's career,
Obscure the sunshine or increase the gloom.

L'AVENIR.

HE drove his coursers down the slope
　　Where Fancy yields to earnest Thought—
Where Reason's claim is tinged with Hope
　　For brighter days, by suff'ring bought,—

For days when nations rush no more
　　To carnage for a bound'ry line;
When plenty smiles on plain and shore,
　　And Arts with rays of glory shine;

When death no longer walks abroad,
　　To sharpen law's half-blunted axe;
Nor alcoholic poison's stored
　　Of self-indulgence, loathsome tax!

No girl shall sell affection's prize;
　　No wife disturb her husband's rest:
Nor children seek, with studied lies,
　　From parents' hands their gold to wrest.

That Future's slope shall glow with light,
　And welcome happy natures then
With visions dear to clearer sight—
　Progressive laws for earnest men.

The Poet crowned shall then be King,
　The Artists circle form his Court,
And those who Nature's secrets bring
　Be welcome to that high resort.

Each clime its tributes offers where
　The Temple of Humanity
Shows, on Time's mount, its columns fair;
　Woman has rights, and Thought is free!

HEAVEN.

CAN Heaven, then, be, as many think,
    A dreamy, waveless rest?
Rather the calm on action's brink,
    Of fullest scope possessed.

The calm of great accomplished fact—
    Of noble purpose done:
Where struggling will has dared to act,
    And manhood's victory won.

Platform whose great perspective lies
    So infinitely true,
That earth an atom seems, which flies
    Across a sphere of blue.

Knowledge, which still explores the roll
    Of deepest human lore,
And finds it but a mimic scroll,
    Fixed to Time's brazen door.

Pleasure, which only sharpened sense
    Can now appreciate,
As it surveys, with joy intense,
    Th' Almighty Mind create.

It sees creation, newly wrought,
    Spring from th' Eternal Will :
In circles to that Centre brought—
    Diverging—blending—still.

No contradictions there are found—
    No passions' ebb and flow :
All objects in harmonious round
    And stateliest measure go.

Those types of goodness, which the heart
    Imperfectly avows,
When musing, from the world apart,
    The soul in silence bows,—

Are *there* unfolded, in the bloom
    Of perfect Nature's grace ;

All lower thoughts the flames consume,
　　That fence God's dwelling place.

Of Contemplation's glories, there
　　The nucleus is found ;
And Action's myriad branches fair,
　　Like faggot's bulk are bound.

All is from all evolved—the light
　　In purest lustre flows ;
What yesterday flashed on the sight,
　　To-day familiar grows.

Of mysteries hid from earth-born eyes,
　　Prophet and bard have seen
Some fragments ; *now*, with glad surprise,
　　They view that Temple's sheen.

FINIS.